Ms. Cassie,

Your encourage
have helped m
Couldn't have done
your assistance.

Adrienne
Johnson-Lee

Rachel

Adrienne Johnson-Lee

ISBN 978-1-63525-064-0 (Paperback)
ISBN 978-1-63525-065-7 (Digital)

Christian Faith Publishing, Inc.
296 Chestnut Street
Meadville, PA 16335
www.christianfaithpublishing.com

Unless otherwise indicated, all scripture quotations are from the King James or the New International Versions of the Bible.

Printed in the United States of America

CONTENTS

Chapter One   The Call, The Mission 3
Chapter Two   Chapel 12
Chapter Three   Can Anything Good Come From Nazareth?....18
Chapter Four   Behind The Old French Doors 27
Chapter Five   Angel's Miracle 32
Chapter Six   The Big Event...38
Chapter Seven   The Adoption 45
Chapter Eight   Mission Possible 56
Chapter Nine   Getting To Know You, Settling In 63
Chapter Ten   Full Circle 71
Chapter Eleven   The Call 77
Chapter Twelve   Simply Smitten..87
Chapter Thirteen Wedding Bells Are Ringing 98
Chapter Fourteen Oh No!...101
Chapter Fifteen   It's A New Season 111

About The Author..116

This book is dedicated to my mother, Reverend Idel Williams, whose tenacity of spirit made a difference in my life. To my papa, Alvin Williams, the most peaceful and gentle spirit on the planet. To Lore, Veronica, Lakisha and Ray, Jr.: your humor and quick wit have helped me so many times. Finally, to my wonderful husband, Raymond. I love you to the moon and back.

A special thank you to every pastor, teacher and professor whose encouragement I value, and to Lisa Renee, who helped make my dream a reality. May you reap a harvest of His blessings.

CHAPTER ONE

The Call, the Mission

Evening subtly approached while hues of red and orange painted the sky. Seems the Creator picked up His paintbrush and crafted something some say they had never before seen. It was the most beautiful canvas, simply beyond compare. The orphanage door opened slightly, allowing the setting sun a momentary place to dwell. Through its cracks, a quiet slightly plump middle-aged woman peeped, displaying the prettiest hazel eyes.

"Good evening. My name is Rachel. How are you?"

"I'm doing great. Pastor Jim is my name. Are you the new volunteer?"

"Yes," she replied. Just as she reached out to shake his hand, the sound of a crying child snatched her attention. There she was, huddled in the corner. "What's the matter?" Rachel asked as she wrapped her arms around the young girl. Her round doe-like eyes met Rachel's.

"I can't find my mommy." She sniffled as though each breath she drew was her last. By then, tears flooded downstream from her doe-like eyes, making pit stops on her chubby cheeks.

Suspicion had begun to set in, and Pastor Jim sensed her desperation. So he chimed in on the conversation. He was known to do that kind of thing.

"Worried about your momma? You needn't be. Somebody will find her. Until then, the Lord will watch over her. You believe that?" Her head bobbed up and down as she quietly agreed.

Now, Rachel was known to be quick on her feet. She knew how to make someone smile in the worst of situations. "I know what we'll do. The old Jamaican woman left some treats in the cupboard. How about a snack?"

"That sounds good," the young girl happily replied. You could sense the relief in her voice. By then, a huge smile replaced the tears, and all seemed well.

As the waves dashed against the shore, nightfall covered the island. Its message was so final: "The Lord's day had ended, and our work done." Rachel climbed into her bunk while whispering a prayer as the young girl eagerly climbed in with her. Though the rules didn't allow that kind of thing, Rachel knew she wouldn't get a wink of sleep otherwise. So they held on to each other until she dozed off.

It had been an exhausting day, and Rachel was feeling empty. Rachel knew she needed some time to regroup. So with her prayer book in hand and a comfy spot upon which to lie, it fell open to the story of Ruth. She read it all, chapter after chapter. Though she had read it many times before, there was something fresh, something new—a heavenly revelation uncovered. Emotion flooded her soul as if a river washed over her. Rachel felt refreshed; she felt reassured. She knew the right decision had been made—that the mission trip was part of God's plan for her and she was in the center of His purposes.

Prior to the trip, Rachel had questions. Was the trip the thing to do? Was it the right place and time? Had she perhaps missed God? Rachel loved to pray and had been fasting half days for weeks. She believed it was the Holy Spirit that pointed her way, that He had orchestrated her answer. *Sometimes people second-guess themselves and try to outthink God, but that never works*, she thought to herself. *He knows the path our lives are to take. Jeremiah 29:11 says, "For I know the plans I have for you," declares the LORD, "plans to prosper you and not to harm you, plans to give you hope and a future."* Those words soothed Rachel to her very core. So much so that when she looked out her window, there was evidence God's hand was again at work, crafting something beautiful. Puffy clouds seemed to sign off and seal the deal that God was at work. They decorated the sky as the sun made its way to her resting place for the day.

Morning met Rachel with a smile, and all was well. Her little angel had been placed in the children's ward, and she wanted to check on her. In her heart, she knew the Lord would make things better for her. After all, He provided for Ruth and Naomi in the midst of some pretty tough times. He was the same God then as He was now and didn't love that little girl any less. As Rachel walked across the field, she sensed the warmth of His love; it felt like the ocean's breeze, almost intoxicating. She whispered a prayer asking Him to order her steps and to speak through her. When she turned the corner, that little girl was standing next to her bunk as if she knew Rachel was coming.

"Good morning," Rachel whispered. "Are you ready for some breakfast?" Her million-dollar smile met no resistance, and into Rachel's arms she ran. It was like her child who was lost had now been found.

The lunchroom was filled with precious little ones, just like that little girl. They all appeared to have good appetites and were no stranger to good eating. By the looks of things, neither was she. She ate and ate and ate. First, she had a hearty helping of fried banana, then she added on some freshly sliced mangoes from the field. Finally, she finished up with a small bowl of hot creamy oatmeal. While she was enjoying her meal, they chatted about all kinds of things. They talked about her favorite foods, her favorite television show, sports, and so much more. Finally, when she seemed comfortable in her new surroundings, Rachel asked about her parents. "What are their names? Where do they live?" The little girl didn't seem to know much beyond their names and where they lived, and Rachel was fine with that. At least now there was something to go on. Since the administrators didn't know a lot about her, staff officially named her Angel. It fit her perfectly, and she didn't seem to mind at all.

Rachel's team leader was supposed to meet with her shortly as she needed to update her on the status of her case load. Ms. Tangy was her name. She was a unique combination of everyone's mother and a drill sergeant. She could quickly gather everyone under her wings like a mother hen, comforting them when needed, then quickly take charge of the situation like mother hens do, shooing off outsiders, keeping her young safe, all in one breath. She had the most unparalleled qualities that made everyone fall in love with her. She was warm, easy to talk to, a great listener, wise, and full of great counsel, along with the tenacity of a bull, all wrapped into one. A fighter she was. There was no denying she was somebody special. For the meeting, Rachel needed her notes, which unfortunately, were in her file cabinet. "Again, I can't believe I forgot them," Rachel mumbled. So off she rushed to gather her things. When she arrived at her quarters, she noticed her journal lying on the bed. Strangely enough, it was open. Now, typically that wasn't something she would have done. Nonetheless, she picked it up and began to read, totally forgetting Ms. Tangy was waiting for her to return.

> "Spiritual maturity is something to be attained. One can never rush the process or

ignore its presence. Time and opportunities are God's proving ground. Don't miss your opportunity."

That's what it said. Her heart was struck in reverence; she somehow knew her Heavenly Father was at work. Seems so long ago when the words came from God's Spirit and onto that page, maybe twelve years or so.

Rachel's life was so different then. She was in a loving relationship with her former spouse. They had the house, two-car garage, and a couple of kids dream under their belts, and all was right with the world. She loved him so; there was no denying it. Their friends thought they were an "ideal couple," or so it seemed. The girls were excelling in school, and it seemed they might have a singer and a gymnast on their hands. Nadia Comanche had recently taken center stage at the Olympics, and their little girl could imitate her to a T. Plus, she had the flexibility, beauty, grace, and strength of a dancer. Saturday after Saturday, Rachel drove her daughter to gymnastics class while her older sister worked with a vocal coach. She was the typical multitasking mom. Either she was busy counseling and praying for people, chaperoning Girl Scout events, hosting roller-skating parties and sleepovers, selling those delicious Girl Scout cookies, or being a wife to her mister. Her to-do list seemed never-ending.

While Rachel was busy multitasking, Trina kept the house tidy and in order. She was the best maid ever. Some say Rachel was borderline OCD, and they're probably right, because she liked a clean house then and she likes a clean house now. Rachel once spent two hours cleaning their self-cleaning stove. She scrubbed, polished, and shined that stainless steel until you could see your reflection, and then beamed with pride. When suddenly and quite out of the blue, her mister's appetite jumped into fourth gear, which meant she'd be cooking up something special, well, the "it girl" in her stood on her tippy toes and said with one hand on her hip, "I'm not fixin' to mess up my clean stove. No, sir. You"ll just have to settle for Burger King!" Surprisingly, he didn't argue but in his gentle way looked up at her, smiled, then proceeded to put on his shoes, and off to Burger King he went. He even brought back a little something special for her.

Rachel sincerely loved the Lord. He had first place in her life. She wouldn't think of beginning or ending her day without honoring him. The Bible was her favorite book. Daily, she spent hours reading it and waiting in His presence for guidance. It was the only life Rachel had ever known, and that was fine by her.

Before she realized it, the years had passed, the girls were off to college, and a new life awaited her. She had lived in the northeast corner of the country her entire life. The four seasons were intriguingly beautiful; each had its own flavor. There was nothing like spring's freshly cut flower–scented air. Warm yet breezy. Summer's heat was brief yet welcomed. Fall displayed leaves of red, green, orange, and brown. Fall foliage is what they called it. The cold, ice, and snow-filled winters were a force to be reckoned with. But it was those nor'easters that cast the final vote; the time had come to relocate to a more comfortable climate. After all, her mister was getting on in age, and Rachel feared each time a nor'easter blew in their direction, he might not survive the clean-up. So after months of praying, planning, and packing, off they went to find their new paths.

Family members joined them on their journey. After three days of travelling, they arrived safely. Moving vans and an entourage of five family-filled vehicles pulled into the cul-de-sac of their new neighborhood. When they walked into their home, they immediately lifted their hands toward heaven and gave thanks. A few phone calls to their folks up north was next on the agenda, then finally, the unloading began. It took a few weeks to get unpacked and settled, and their new lives began. Like the changing of the four seasons made an impact on their lives, so did their current state of affairs. Everything was different, especially the cold weather they'd left behind for warmer, more stable temperatures.

The first major task was to find a new church to attend. Rachel and her mister looked and looked. Finally, they heard Pastor Quartermain would be conducting a financial seminar at a nearby church. He was senior pastor at Healing Ministries of New York and had quite a following, nationally and internationally. So they found their way to the seminar. They had been praying about a place of worship, and it sure felt like home. So there is where they placed their roots. It was a great church, and the girls fell in love with it too. God's favor surrounded their family. Life couldn't seem more perfect. Promotion was in the air. They were at the right place at the right time, then something happened.

* * *

"Whew, another flashback!" Rachel was suddenly jerked back into the reality of the present. "Why would I be thinking on that? It's been so long ago." She didn't have an answer but knew in time the answer would be revealed.

The meeting! Tangy! Oh my goodness! Rachel ran as quickly as her feet would carry her. "Ms. Tangy, please forgive me. I was momentarily detained."

Angrily, she mumbled, "I'll say you were. The meeting ended half an hour ago. The chores are posted, and your new assignment is listed."

"Yes, ma'am," Rachel reverently replied.

"Oh, by the way, more bodies have been found. The morgue contacted the office. You need to go see what's going on."

"The morgue," Rachel screamed under her breath. "That's not what I had in mind!" The hurricane had been a beast, and half the island was without power. Many lives were lost, and the death toll still rising. She felt unprepared, but the call to the mission field was strong, and Rachel could not deny its presence. "Dear Lord, I didn't think it would require all of this. I could use some help, please." She didn't want to go but realized this was part of the process.

The township officials got a hold of some dental records and helped Pastor Jim locate photos of the orphans' parents, and they located Angel's parents too.

She dreaded the ride. It seemed never ending. The narrow, winding, mud-covered roads were unstable, and she was afraid to look down for fear of what would be revealed. Would there be pieces of bodies mixed in with debris or some other terrible thing? Only time would reveal, and Rachel wasn't exactly rushing things along. Upon arrival, the undertaker welcomed Rachel. He was quite cheerful. When that's your regular line of work, dealing with death is just another day's work to you. He explained the bodies had been discovered earlier and had not yet been claimed or prepared for burial. He led her into the refrigerated room. It was cold. The stench of death was strong and distasteful, and she wanted no part of it. Drawer after drawer, body after body, no one seemed to fit their description. Finally, they found Angel's parents. Their storm-beaten remains were evidence of the death blow the island suffered. The sight was disturbing; she felt sick to her stomach and had to run out to relieve herself. Within seconds, it was accompanied by dizziness and lightheadedness. She felt faint and had to take a seat. The undertaker was gracious and put smelling salts under her nose to prevent anything further from happening.

Documents had to be completed by the next of kin and staff only knew about Angel. So Rachel took them back with her to the orphanage. She cried all the way. She didn't have a clue how to break the news to Angel.

After supper, Angel seemed happy. Spaghetti was on the menu. What child doesn't like spaghetti? Judging from her appearance, she had a plate or two. She had sauce stains all over her hands and face and looked a fright. Rachel helped her get cleaned up. After her bath, she gave her some "big girl" lotion to wear so she would smell pretty. Angel loved that. As Rachel tucked her into bed, she said, fighting back tears, "Angel, the Lord has allowed your mom and dad to fall asleep for a while. But when they awake, they'll be in heaven with Jesus." Her precious little face was flooded with tears as she laid her head between Rachel's breasts. She could feel the weight of Angel's sorrow and didn't know what else to say. As she opened her mouth, the Holy Spirit sang through her, "Yes, Jesus loves me." Rachel sang and rocked Angel in her arms for hours until she fell asleep.

Rachel hardly slept at all that night, tossing and turning in her bunk; Angel was on her mind. Rachel had loved children all her life, taught Sunday school, and even led youth groups too. But this was totally different from any other experience—something new, something different. Rachel ached inside and wanted to sense the presence of the Holy Spirit, to be held in His arms and reassured she was on track with His plan for her life. In the quietness of the hour, Rachel knew He was near. The words of Psalms 23 repeated over and over in her mind. She wept until tears met under her chin. It was then she realized His purposes for her life were being revealed. It was sobering.

Morning arrived, and the sun made her appearance. A new day had dawned, and there was work to be done.

CHAPTER TWO

Chapel

The Open Arms Orphanage was fairly well concealed, tucked neatly into a gully on Saint Michael's Avenue behind an old green building covered in moss. The sloping ground was paved with native stones, where grass peaked through its cracks, grasping for moisture and sunlight. The main floor wasn't at all modern. Curtains and odd sheets substituted for walls that didn't exist, and to catch a breath of fresh air, staff members had to crank out old windows and wait for the ocean's breeze to come and refresh them.

Six weeks passed since Hurricane Diane devastated the island, and orphanage officials had yet to locate any other next of kin who could help Angel out. The island had very different laws, especially when it came to burying the dead. Unable to hold their remains any longer, the mortician was forced to cremate Angel's parents.

Now Angel had become the darling of us all. Yet, everyone wanted to give her parents the sendoff they deserved and one Angel would always remember. Since the care of the orphans was the main responsibility, it was decided waiting till after supper was the way to go. The children would be freshly fed, calm, and soon ready to retire, plus summer evenings were decorated with beautifully lit skies until about eight and would provide the illumination needed.

Everyone gathered at Kate's Bay and stood in a large circle as Pastor Jim read his favorite scripture. Angel had quickly taken a liking to Jamaica's Kate's Bay; she could be found playing in its white sand or washing her feet in the warm blue waters on a regular basis. As the orphan's choir rang their bells—a tender rendition of "We Are All God's Friend"—the sun went to sleep. The stars peeped through the night's silky sky as they flung their ashes toward the heavens. Amazingly, the stars twinkled as if to say, *Welcome to eternal rest*. It felt like heaven bowed down and kissed the earth.

Now Angel seemed oblivious to the details of the tragedy. She buried herself in her schoolwork, and everyone was happy about it. Her hefty appetite got heftier, adding pounds to her frail frame, and inches too. She was growing like freshly cut grass soaked from the rain. She appeared to be okay, enjoying her friends from the orphanage and adjusting to her new surroundings. But it soon became apparent there was something else going on.

Angel had been examined when she arrived at the orphanage and had gone through some routine blood work too. It wasn't anything out of the ordinary because such was the custom with all the children. Unfortunately, the results revealed some disturbing news. Seems Angel was eight weeks along. She was pregnant. "How could this have happened? She's only eleven years old!" Rachel screamed within. Rachel felt every emotion possible. Anger boiled up inside, and her hands shook uncontrollably. It was no longer anger but rage in its rarest form. She could not believe what she was hearing. Angel was such a fragile thing, kind of clingy you could say. Her voice was so soft that when she spoke, you could barely hear what she was saying. Guess you could say she was a special child who had special ways. As Rachel managed to calm herself a bit, thoughts of what Angel's future would be like flooded her mind. What were they going to do? Had the orphanage dealt with this kind of thing before? What was to happen next? Rachel couldn't come to terms with any of the answers.

During the next few weeks, Angel developed a strong liking to chapel. It seemed to intrigue her. She loved being surrounded by older people; some were at least three times her age. It was obvious she found comfort in their care because when they talked with her, she seemed calmer than usual. Almost like their time together was some type of anesthetic. She watched every move they made as if it were her roadmap to happiness and wholeness. She moved her lips in sync with theirs, singing loudly and, on many occasions, out of tune as if it were the normal thing to do.

Now, chapel was a special time where the staff and volunteers gathered and fellowshipped gaily with each other. It was a great time to get refreshed from the day's work, and Lord knows it was needed. Since everyone's days were filled with patching up the sick, solving problems, and keeping folks sane, getting together for chapel was the perfect opportunity to put aside concerns and be reminded of the good things the Lord had planned for the future. Pastor Jim was just five feet eleven inches tall, weighing in at about 160 pounds of pure muscle. It was evident he spent a great deal of time at the gym when he was back home in the US, and a great deal of time studying Scripture too. When he opened his mouth, wonderful words of wisdom flowed. He could preach like nobody's business. His voice would rise and fall at the right places, bringing everyone to their feet, and they loved every minute of it.

Now, it was mandatory that each volunteer participate in the chapel service, and the choices were few. Either you lead prayer, read a scripture, ministered the word, or served as an armor bearer. Rachel liked working in the background and tried her best to avoid the preaching, public speaking thing. She felt comfortable serving behind the scenes and was perfectly happy letting someone else do the other stuff.

However, this morning was different. Sun and clouds filled the sky. The winds whistled, and the atmosphere testified of His might and power. Psalms 19:1 (NIV) says, "The heavens declare the glory of God; the skies proclaim the work of His hands." God's presence was evident. You could sense it in the air. Hands were lifted; hearts were tender. Rough and raspy voices had an angelic tone, as though there was one voice only. Many voices blended to become one, and everyone had one thing on their minds. Everyone seemed eager to feel His holy presence. That alone would sooth the hunger of their hearts, and Angel was quietly sitting next to Rachel, taking it all in.

Now she wasn't your typical eleven-year-old. She reminded Rachel so much of herself when she was that age—bubbly, warm, and welcoming. She would trust just about anyone and had a glow about her even when things weren't going just right.

Her hands were raised in praise as tears hung on her chubby cheeks like drops of joy. Pastor Jim noticed her. His sensitivity to the Holy Spirit was always on point. You could tell he felt His holy presence. There was Holy Spirit anticipation in the air. People were praising the Lord, stirring all kinds of commotion, rocking and swaying to the music. Guess you can say they were excited. Just as things were settling down, Pastor Jim lifted his hands and belted, "I feel the Holy Spirit's prompting. Rachel, I believe you have something to say. Come and minister." Her jaw dropped. To say she was shocked would be a major understatement. Rachel hadn't prepared herself to speak, and her nerves went into overload. As she stepped to the podium, she caught a glimpse of Angel sitting in the audience. Upon her was a heavenly glow an intense radiance, as though the light of glory shone on her. In that very moment, Rachel received fresh revelation of God's love for His children. As she opened her mouth to speak, words began to flow that she wasn't aware were in her vocabulary. It was frightening yet refreshing. Ten minutes later, the altar was filled, and many were on their knees weeping. Rachel doesn't remember much else except it was a powerful yet pivotal moment. Something had changed, and she knew the course of her life would never be the same.

As Rachel took her seat, a call came across the intercom that Ms. Tangy needed help in administration. There were intercoms in every part of the facility, even in the chapel. So duty called, and off she went. Seems there was always something to be done, and her nursing degree certainly came in handy. Now Rachel's chore list was especially long, and she needed to complete hospital rounds too. In Ms. Tangy's opinion, the team members were her "busy beavers," and they giggled every time she would say it.

When they bumped into each other in the hallway of the children's ward, they got to talking. Ms. Tangy had to miss out on chapel because of some kind of emergency and wanted to get caught up on the happenings. They talked and talked about an hour before realizing what they had done. Ms. Tangy was like everyone's mother; she had a sixth sense about things. She knew when something was wrong, when one of her babies was in trouble.

Rachel hadn't felt like herself since she got word about the passing of Angel's parents, that they perished in the storm. Her heart ached at the thought of Angel's uncertain future. She would take Angel home with her in a heartbeat, but she had a brother who wasn't too fond of children. He was at home in the States, making sure things were stable while Rachel was away. They inherited their grandmother's place after she passed on. It was an old Victorian house where hidden behind the old French doors were years of family secrets, and they did their best to keep those things quiet. He, a six-foot-four 250-pound ex-marine, had picked up a few strange habits along the way. Rachel couldn't imagine how he would respond to a child living with them, playing and making all kinds of mess along the way. What was she to do?

Now, Ms. Tangy was no stranger to such cases and possessed old-fashioned wisdom like nobody's business. She held out her arms, and into them Rachel fell like a little child. The warmth of her love comforted her as she prayed for God's guidance. "What would I do without you?" cried Rachel. Ms. Tangy simply smiled and said, "Wisdom's way will work," as she rubbed Rachel's back then quietly walked away. *What does that mean?* Rachel thought to herself. It was just like Ms. Tangy to drop a bombshell like that and then walk off like nothing had been said. Now Rachel was left to do the work of trying to figure that one out.

By now, Rachel had been a nurse some thirteen years. Some say she was a natural because she loved people and treated them like kin. They were just a few months into their tour of duty and had experienced so much. At times, Rachel felt more like a social worker than a missionary, but she loved every minute of it. She had somehow evaded the call to the mission field for some time though. One thing or another always got in the way. But her opportunity had finally arrived, and she was thrilled. Grandma used to say, "When you wait on the Lord, things will happen when the time is right." And yes, Rachel had to agree. They did!

CHAPTER THREE

Can Anything Good Come from Nazareth?

Now Angel was growing and glowing. Pregnancy certainly agreed with her. Pastor Jim and Rachel decided it was time to have a little talk with her about it. So they called her into the office where Ms. Tangy, Rachel, and Pastor Jim were waiting to hear her story.

"Angel, how are you feeling these days?" asked Pastor Jim.

"I'm feeling okay, I guess," she quietly uttered.

"Do you know what is happening to you? There's a baby growing inside your belly," Rachel recounted.

"Yes, Ms. Rachel. My cousin had a baby, and her tummy grew just like mine," she said in a monotone-like voice, almost without feeling or emotion. "She had a baby boy, but he died 'cause he was too small. That's what the midwife told her."

"Sweetheart, do you know who did this to you?" asked Rachel. "Yes, ma'am. It wasn't supposed to happen. I kept telling him no, but he wouldn't listen," Angel replied as her voice began to tremble.

Rachel recounted, "Are you saying he forced himself on you?"

"Does that mean he made me do it?" the girl responded.

"Yes, that's what I'm saying," exclaimed Rachel.

"It was my father's brother. He's just a few years older than me. He's kind of strong 'cause he works in the fields and plays soccer most days. Sometimes, when he comes around, we would play soccer. That's how I learned how to play. One day before the storm, he came by to talk to Mummy. He told me weeks earlier that he wanted to start an all-girls soccer team and wanted me to join. But my parents weren't home. So we started playing hide-n-seek while Mummy and Daddy were getting supplies from town. He said, 'Come to the shed. I've got carrot juice for you. It will quench your thirst.' So I did. When I stepped inside the shed, he grabbed me, covered my mouth, and threw me down on some hay. That's when it happened. It hurt. I'd never done that before. I tried to scream, but he threatened he'd do it to me again and again. The smell of the field was on him. It sickened me. I wanted to vomit. I was afraid it would never end, so I kept quiet while he did his business." Angel's quivering voice expressed sadness almost unimaginable as her eyes released a fountain of tears.

Rachel's heart ached as she listened to the story. She did her best to remain calm and professional, but it wasn't easy. She had visions of choking him to within an inch of his life. That's what flashed through her mind.

"Does he know you're having a baby?" asked Pastor Jim with eyebrows raised and a scowl on his face.

"No, sir. He was with Mummy and Daddy when the storm hit. I haven't seen him since." Ms. Tangy, however, had a look of resolve, like she had it all worked out in her mind.

There was so much to be discussed, but they didn't want to press Angel. After all, she had already had a heaping helping of heartache, and they didn't want to add to that equation. So Rachel walked her back to the dorm, where she took a few moments to comfort her.

It took Rachel a while to walk back. She knew Pastor Jim and Ms. Tangy had plenty they wanted to say. So when she arrived back at the office, Ms. Tangy quietly said, "Stopped for a snack, did ya?"

"No, I didn't. I don't have much of an appetite right now, and Angel didn't either, which is not her norm you know. What's on your mind? You've got that look again," asked Rachel.

"I don't want to say just yet," Ms. Tangy replied.

"Her uncle! Can you believe that? I'm just furious!" yelled Rachel. Ms. Tangy sat quietly as Rachel ranted on and on. "What do you think of that? We've got to contact the authorities. After all, she is just eleven. She's a minor! What was he thinking?"

"Well, obviously he wasn't doing much thinking," said Ms. Tangy. "Let's let it rest for the day. Perhaps tomorrow she'll give us a description and a bit more information."

"Yes," replied Rachel. "That sounds like a good idea."

Now, the nearest midwife was on the other side of the island. It would take them hours to get to her. The town doctor only had limited experience in prenatal care and birthing babies because midwives were everyone's favorite. "Ms. Tangy, I just thought of the prenatal class held over at St. Augustine's on Tuesday nights. They teach the women how to breastfeed and about changing diapers, stuff like that. Do you know what the criteria is? Is Angel too young to attend?" asked Rachel.

"I'm not sure about the age requirement, but I'll make a phone call or two. I'll let you know later."

"Thanks, Ms. Tangy."

Would she consider adoption? Would she abort the baby? Who would provide for the child? So many questions were bouncing around in Rachel's mind, and she didn't have any answers.

About two hours later, as Rachel was about to turn in for the day, she noticed someone's shadow out of the corner of her eye. It was Angel. She loved stuff animals, and her collection included the cutest pink elephant. As she held on to her stuffed elephant, she whispered, "Ms. Rachel, I need to tell you something." Rachel's heart nearly jumped out of her chest with fear. What else could she have to say? Wearing her best smile, she said, "What is it, Angel?"

"Ms. Rachel, while he was doing his business on top of me, he said he'd done it before to some of the boys from the soccer team."

By now, the shock of it all had begun to settle in, or at least that's what Rachel thought. *What, another added twist? Dear Jesus!* She took a deep breath, trying to maintain what was left of her calm demeanor and proceeded to listen to the details. "Angel, are you sure that's what he said?"

"Yes, ma'am. He said the boys didn't like it either," she related while wearing a tear-stained face. *Dear God!* Rachel thought under her breath. "Okay. That's enough for now, Angel. We can talk about that later if you like."

"Yes, ma'am," she replied.

"Are you alright? Come, let me give you another hug. Don't fret yourself. Everything is going to be alright. You believe that?"

"Yes, ma'am," Angel replied. "Okay, let me walk you back to your room." While they walked together, neither of them had much to say. In fact, there was dead silence. There wasn't even the sound of a fly buzzing about. Rachel could only imagine what was going through Angel's mind right about now. She knew what was on her mind. Rachel wanted to find him and well, let your imagination finish that sentence. When they finally arrived, from what seemed like a walk lasting an eternity, she gave Angel another hug, said a prayer, and tucked her in for the night.

By now, Rachel's shock had deepened. "Dear Lord, my heart simply cannot handle another shocking detail!" Now, whether the Lord heard that prayer or not, Rachel could not say for certain. But she certainly hoped so. The shock and disbelief was beginning to take its toll on her. She couldn't think, her appetite just about vanished, and she wasn't getting very much sleep.

The walk back to the hospital seemed longer than usual. Normally, she could clock that path in less than five minutes. But tonight, it seemed never ending.

"Ms. Tangy, you'll never believe what just happened." As Rachel replayed the event, Ms. Tangy's mouth dropped in disbelief. "Do you know what this now means?"

"Yes, ma'am. Angel could have been exposed to an STD. They can be pretty dangerous you know." Rachel screamed within! Ms. Tangy looked at her with one eyebrow raised and said, "Remember when you asked me earlier if something was going on?"

"Yes," Rachel replied. "Well, one of her tests came back showing some type of abnormality."

"Oh no. What type?"

"Well, it was inconclusive. We'll need to do further testing to determine exactly what it is," replied Ms. Tangy.

"When? How soon?" There was a sense of urgency in Rachel's voice as you might imagine.

Neither of them got much sleep that night. Their thoughts were on Angel, and with good reason too. Before Rachel knew it, the morning's sun peeped through the skies and a new day dawned. Her top priority, of course, was getting Angel scheduled for testing. Now, Pastor Jim hadn't heard the latest bomb that dropped, and neither of them was anxious about being the first to tell him. After all, he had the care of the parishioners on his mind as well, and a burden they didn't want to be.

Angel's presence in the classroom, her growing belly, soon became the topic of discussion. Everyone was whispering, and Rachel was becoming concerned how it might affect her.

"Angel, how was school today?"

"Fine, ma'am. My classmates tease me 'bout my belly. I don't mind 'cause I know why," she said.

"Do you think they understand why?" asked Rachel.

"I don't know, but if they ask, I'll tell them," Angel replied.

"You are such a brave girl. Where do you get it from?" Rachel asked.

"During chapel, Pastor Jim told us to trust God no matter what. That's who helps me. When I lay down at night, I think about what happened to me. It makes me sad, and sometimes I cry. But when I say my prayers, I ask the Lord to help me be brave, and He does."

"Angel, I'm so proud of you. You're so courageous. Seems it was just yesterday when Pastor Jim preached about Jesus, the carpenter's son. He said the Pharisees didn't believe Jesus was the Messiah, a Prophet sent from God, because he was from Nazareth. Nazareth had a bad reputation, and folks said nothing good could ever come from such an evil place. When John the Baptist tried to convince the people otherwise, they still didn't believe."

"Yes, ma'am, I remember," replied Angel.

"Angel, you remind me of that story," said Rachel.

"How?" the girl replied.

"Well, seems you've had your share of difficult situations. Your mummy and daddy went to heaven, your uncle wasn't very nice to you, and now you've got a little one growing in your belly. In spite of all those things, I believe something good is going to happen for you. I believe you're going to be somebody very special. Maybe even a missionary!"

"Oh, Ms. Rachel, I would love that!" Angel beamed with joy while wearing her famous million-dollar smile.

Now, Ms. Tangy got word Nurse Bonnie would be arriving on Wednesday to retest Angel, and Rachel was just a bundle of nerves. Her stomach was tied in knots. Ms. Tangy, however, was as steady as always. She never seemed to get too upset about anything no matter how horrible the situation.

Nurse Bonnie had a long list of orphans to treat. A few cases of chicken pox, a sprained ankle, and a broken finger were the worst of them. She was quick and thorough. People knew if Nurse Bonnie was on duty, they wouldn't have to be sitting around a long time. She could fix folks up with the speed of lightning; some say in record time.

Reliving such an event would drain the poor girl dry, thought Rachel. So she suggested Angel take the day off from school. It had been emotionally draining for her, and she needed to be refreshed before trying to return to her studies. So off they went to visit the chapel for a brief time of prayer. Then they stopped by the kitchen for their usual hearty breakfast. Lord knows nothing seems to slow down that appetite of hers. She would say, "I'm eating for two." However, Rachel often wondered if it was two linebackers or two chubby ballerinas.

By now, Nurse Bonnie had tended to her list of patients and was ready to see Angel. So again, the intercom got put to good use. "Angel," Nurse Bonnie beckoned, "please come to my cubicle." Angel scurried along, finding her way into her cubicle. Nurse Bonnie had the patience of a saint and could make any illness sound so minimal. So she proceeded to explain Angel's situation, showed some videos, and then administered the test.

Rachel watched as Nurse Bonnie answered Angel's questions. She was so gentle towards her.

A week went by, and they hadn't heard any news. As usual, Rachel was fretting a bit, but Angel was calm and steady. Maybe her present state was the result of the chapel service they had just attended, Rachel couldn't say for sure. But, she was calm, and she was steady.

"Ms. Rachel, something good is going to come of this, remember?"

"Yes, sweetheart, you're right. It is."

Now Pastor Jim and Ms. Tangy were meeting in Pastor Jim's office and sent word that Angel and Rachel should come to his office immediately. There was such a sense of urgency in the messenger's tone. Anxiety began to build within and decided to find its resting place in Rachel's throat.

"Angel, let's take a walk. I'm in need of some fresh air, aren't you?" asked Rachel while her voice trembled.

"Alright, ma'am, if you say so," Angel replied.

As Angel and Rachel walked the path, they held each other's hands and sang funny songs she learned at the orphanage. Rachel wasn't willing to reveal her true feelings and fears; she didn't want them to affect her Angel. As they approached the building, there was such peace and calm in the air. It washed over Rachel like a fresh soaking rain. Fear was gone, and a new dose of faith took its place.

"Angel, would you please sit for a minute?" asked Nurse Bonnie.

"Yes, ma'am, I can."

In her hand was a brown envelope. She turned to Ms. Rachel and the others and said, "Angel has tested positive for the HIV virus. However, we're not certain if the fetus has been affected." A quiet hush came over the room as tears ran down Rachel's face. Ms. Tangy sat quietly in her chair almost motionless. Pastor Jim took a deep breath and then exhaled. Their responses spoke volumes, and Angel knew something serious had just occurred. However, her courage surpassed anything ever expected of her.

"Something good will come of this. Remember, Ms. Rachel? Something good will come of this."

CHAPTER FOUR

Behind the Old French Doors

Now Rachel's grandma was famous for wearing colorful aprons. It was part of who she was. She was only four feet eleven inches tall and had the clearest skin anyone could wish for. She got up every morning and washed her face with white cream in the dark blue jar sold by the local drug store. It smelled like some kind of peppermint, can't remember what it was called, but it seemed to work for her. She loved it and often wore it as a mask during the day, scaring us young'uns half to death! Then she would put on her apron of the day. Her pastel bib-style aprons fit her tiny frame to a tee and became her uniform of choice. She wore them on laundry day, shopping day, cleaning day, canning day, and any other day you could think of. She loved their home and took great pride in its appearance, especially the old French doors that connected each room. She would polish those doors till you could immediately spot your reflection. She loved their home and their family with a passion unsurpassed. She was always storing up some kind of surprise. She loved making them laugh and smile at each other. However, tucked away in each apron pocket were a fable, a story, and part of the family's history that only she could tell in the fluidity of her tender tones.

It was no secret; Rachel came from a long line of deeply religious people who went to church all the time. Sunday, Tuesday, Friday, and Saturday, and that was when a revival wasn't in town. If a revival was in town, they would go every night, and all day Sunday too.

Since the days of slavery, Rachel's people told stories and preached in cotton fields, under shade trees, and in old wooden buildings they called The Church House. The stories of their past were filled with scriptures, courtships, humor, deep, dark, and sometimes dirty secrets. But Grandma had them all safely tucked away in her memory, filed in perfect order, chapter by chapter. With her cup of coffee in hand, she would belt out, "Your great auntie Vi had on a blue dress the day of the awful storm of 19 and 32. It was full of white specks around her neck and on the tail," all while enjoying her cup of Sanka, as no other brand of coffee would do. She loved it and kept a jar of it hidden in her secret stash of goodies. With each sip, she would continue telling her story, never missing any part of its detail. She had a memory like no one Rachel had ever known before, and she was lucky enough to have had it passed down to her.

However, unlike Grandma, Rachel had no apron pocket or safe place to hide her secrets. So she buried them deep within where nobody could find them. They were her private property and belonged to no one but her.

For instance, when she was just eight years old, her mom had a day job working at a local retail store. She wore shirtwaist dresses; they were the thing of her day. Fitted to the waist with full bottom skirts, she would accentuate her tiny waste with her favorite belt. Wearing her green smock labeled Mrs. James, she officially took to her duties. She enjoyed her work and the discounts employees earned as a result. She was always buying Rachel pretty dresses and things. Back then, little girls wore dresses most of or all the time, even when playing outdoors. The tough part was, their knees looked like a war zone, just horrible. They wore the scars of every fall, scrape, and mosquito bite they had ever experienced. Things were so different back then. Children could walk to school alone without fear of being kidnapped. People looked out for each other, and their landlady, Mrs. Grey, was one of those generous, kind-hearted ones. She knew Rachel's mom worked a full-time job, so she volunteered her teenage son to babysit her during the afternoons. It seemed the right thing to do, and Rachel's mom agreed. What Mrs. Grey didn't know was her son wasn't behaving; he was touching Rachel. It was inappropriate, and she was too young to understand the seriousness of the matter. It was uncomfortable, and she didn't like it. But he never listened to her nos. Seemed he thought Rachel was saying yes. When she grew older, she realized what he had done to her, but she somehow found the strength to move on. She survived, and eventually, their family moved to another city. Then it happened again.

Rachel's mom and Stepfather became preachers who, over time, gained a bit of influence among the congregants of their church. They had a trusted circle of friends who they loved. Now, at the time, she was just fourteen and attending the local high school and needed to earn some extra cash. So she prayed and prayed that the Lord would give her a job. Suddenly, an opportunity arose. It was the answer to her prayers, or so she thought. The church deacon and his wife came to her and asked her to help out, that he and his wife no longer had a sitter for their children. It appeared to be a reasonable request and something she could do, so Rachel agreed and soon began her new job. It seemed safe, that is until the good deacon tried to touch her in inappropriate places. He wanted more than any babysitter should give. She immediately tried to get away from him, but he would not relent. So, she escaped his advances by running out of their home. When others asked why, she never told anyone the real reason for it. She just complained to her mom that she had too much homework and needed extra time to keep up. That was one time she was so thankful she was a student, because it was the best excuse ever. Her mother never questioned her reasoning. However, the good deacon knew the truth and begged her to keep quiet about it. Back in the day, caller ID hadn't yet been invented, and when he called, she became petrified and fearful. Again and again, he begged her not to tell anyone, so she promised she wouldn't. Rachel was young and naive and did not want to hurt his wife. They had built a special bond; she was like a mentor, the big sister she never had, and Rachel didn't want to mess things up. Plus, she knew the truth would rip her to pieces, so she kept quiet.

By the time she reached adulthood, her memory was filled with painful disdain. Now, Rachel could easily identify and empathize with what Angel was feeling. From the well of emotions buried deep within, she pulled out her best and offered Angel the love she so deserved. Angel was such a grateful little lamb.

By now, it had been years since Grandma left them. She is resting in the arms of Jesus. When Rachel thinks of Grandma polishing those old French doors, she is reminded behind them is where secrets were stored. But more importantly, that is also where love was shown, where babies were born, where Bible verses were learned, and where music could be heard.

Rachel never told her mom any part of that story or what happened to her. She let those secrets stay hidden behind the old French doors, where they are quietly resting.

Now, whenever she goes home and walks into that old Victorian home, she automatically thinks of Grandma and her apron filled with stories. She thinks of the damp cold basement and the musty memory-filled attic where Grandma's old trunks rest by the chimney. "I don't know why things happen the way they do, but I'm assured God's plans are perfect, because He makes things new and beautiful in His time," whispered Rachel in a gentle tone.

CHAPTER FIVE

Angel's Miracle

Angel seemed so uncomfortable. Her swollen ankles and ever-growing belly looked as though she was carrying either one very big baby or a couple of linebackers. Though she wasn't due for at least another six weeks, all signs pointed towards an early appearance of the new addition. Team members got together and volunteered to keep a close watch on her, checking on her every hour or so. She loved the attention and the special treats too. The Old Jamaican women catered to her, fulfilling all her special cravings, pickles and ice cream were among her favorites.

This particular day, the ocean's breeze was cool and inviting, and Rachel wanted to explore its pleasures. So she asked Angel to come along for a stroll. They walked up and down the beach as sand peeped through their toes. It was a beautiful Monday afternoon, intoxicatingly so. However, Rachel's watch suddenly alarmed, halting their time of leisure, alerting them lunchtime had arrived.

By now, the Old Jamaican women had prepared something special. The aroma was inviting and made it easy for them to just follow the scent. Now, her cooking skills always published interesting hints of what was to come. She had a special touch when it came to the kitchen, and it was evident each time Rachel stepped on the scale. As they arrived and saw the crowded dining room, they managed to squeeze into their usual spots. Rachel watched as Angel tore into her plate of food. She scoffed down several jerk chicken wings along with a side of rice and peas, washing it down with a cool glass of carrot juice. "That girl has some kind of appetite!" blurted Rachel while onlookers quietly giggled.

As they rose from the table, Angel made a loud noise, sort of like a grunt. Rachel thought nothing of it as she had just eaten a hearty meal. *Perhaps she was burping*, she thought. But when Angel fell forward, Rachel knew something had gone wrong. Could she be in labor? Had something else happened? Perhaps it was a case of appendicitis? Rachel wasn't certain, so she called for help.

Ms. Tangy had somehow gotten the midwife to stop by the village earlier that day. They guessed the clinic had a few expectant mothers in need of routine care, and an outbreak of chicken pox to spice up matters. Thank goodness she was nearby. Midwife Bette was her name. She was a tall, slender woman with coal black hair straight as a board. It was always neatly pulled back in a ponytail with the prettiest red bow tied to keep it in place. She was a quiet kind of woman, tending to her patients so gingerly. Everyone loved her because she had a good reputation and she knew how to birth babies.

When they arrived, Midwife Bette was waiting by the hospital entrance. "Let's get her onto a gurney, and I'll take a look see." All the while, Angel's countenance turned every shade of grey possible. She moaned and groaned, twisted and turned. You could see the intensity of her pain. It was evident something was wrong.

"How long has she been this way?"

"Well, she seemed fine until right after lunch. That's when she screamed and nearly frightened me to death!" Midwife Bette and Rachel"s conversation continued for a bit. After all, Angel was feeling some type of way, or at least that's what her countenance said. "Ms. Tangy drove the van. We got her here as quickly as we could. Is she gonna be alright?" asked Rachel in a weepy yet frightened voice.

As Midwife Bette tried her best to comfort Angel, she seemed more uncomfortable than ever. "This might sting a bit, just hold on to Ms. Rachel's hand, and you'll be alright. Okay?" said the midwife as the anesthesia-filled needle melted into Angel's flesh.

"Yes, Midwife Bette, I'll try," a brave Angel responded.

She squealed each time the midwife tried to examine her. "Angel, you must trust me. Okay?" So Angel took a few deep breaths and held on for dear life. By then, the anesthesia was beginning to calm her a bit. "From the looks of it, our miracle baby wants to make an early appearance!" said the midwife.

"I knew it!" yelled Rachel with a huge smile in her voice.

"She's already six centimeters dilated!" exclaimed the midwife. Unsatisfied though, she could sense there was an added element to the equation. So she examined her further, and her suspicions were true. There it was, the cord was wrapped around the baby's neck. "Try not to push, even when it feels like you need to. Okay?"

"Yes, ma'am," replied an anxious Angel as her voice trembled. Holding on to Rachel's hand, Angel squeezed and squeezed until Rachel's hand practically went numb. "It hurts, Ms. Rachel!" she screamed. "I know, Angel, but it won't hurt much longer," Rachel said while wiping the sweat from Angel's brow.

Midwife Bette worked for the next ten minutes to unravel the cord. It wasn't an easy task because Angel was just a child and not fully developed. "Rachel, please hold her tightly while I administer a bit more anesthesia. Can you?"

"By all means," an anxious Rachel replied. Again, the conversation was straight and to the point because the midwife had her hands full trying to unravel the cord from the baby's neck. Midwife Bette proceeded to place the mask over Angel's nose, administering a much-needed dose of anesthesia. Finally, she was able to gain access and unwind the cord. Rachel, you might imagine, let out a big sigh of relief. "Thank goodness! Angel, you were a trouper. I'm so proud of you." Angel smiled and lay quietly, trying to regain her strength. She knew though the emergency was over, there was more work to be done, and that her baby had yet to make its grand entrance.

Rachel immediately took on the posture of expectant parent even though she was not. She paced back and forth and back and forth some more. Ms. Tangy could not stand the suspense and took to the chapel to say a few much-needed prayers. Three hours and thirty-five minutes worth of prayer and pacing helped produce someone very special. Rachel beamed with joy while happiness penetrated her every action, her every move. "Angel, you birthed that baby with the strength of an ox," exclaimed Rachel in a voice whose pitch could not go any higher.

Now, their Angel had an angel of her own! Ten fingers, ten toes, curly black hair, and a mocha complexion to match that of her mother's. She weighed in at seven pounds fourteen ounces, and twenty-two inches long—the evidence of all Angel's cravings wrapped up into one beautiful bundle of joy.

Their new addition wasted no time but immediately went for her mother's breast, and it soon became obvious—she had inherited her mother's appetite. Rachel watched in amazement how naturally the whole thing went. The baby ate and burped without hesitation like an old pro, while Angel took a liking to motherhood right away, rocking her, kissing her, and loving on her in the most endearing way.

A few days passed as Angel and her angel rested. All seemed well with the world, and no one was thinking about the obvious. Was the baby HIV positive or not? It felt so good to just enjoy a few days of happiness. After all, hurricane Diane claimed the lives of both of Angel's parents, then she discovered she was pregnant and HIV positive. Couldn't they just pretend everything else was fine?

A week went by, and Angel and her angel were adjusting quite nicely to each other. Though no one wanted to dwell on it, the obvious needed to be dealt with. So Rachel and Ms. Tangy took the necessary steps and got on with the testing. As the closest adult authority in Angel's life, Rachel called the physician and nurse requesting the baby be tested. As they pricked the new addition, Rachel cringed in fear of what could be. She hated having to cause any kind of discomfort to the baby, but it had to be done.

Ten days went by, and Angel and her angel were still in the hospital. Angel was doing well; her recovery was right on schedule. However, on day 7, her condition suddenly changed. She began hemorrhaging and lost a great deal of blood. Now, blood supplies on the island were nearly nonexistent. The hurricane's wounded placed a huge demand on what little they ha and nearly wiped out the limited medical supplies on hand. Angel was RH negative, not the most common blood type there is. So Rachel, Pastor Jim, and Ms. Tangy prayed and prayed for a miracle. They prayed the blood bank would be able to help, and thankfully, they did.

The blood transfusion left Angel feeling weak, and that was to be expected. The doctors didn't seem too concerned and suggested she begin her treatment, which consisted of a cocktail of pills, some of which were large enough to choke a horse. All else aside, Angel's angel was blossoming. Everyone treated her like she was royalty, like she was their very own.

Another day passed as Rachel, Pastor Jim, and Ms. Tangy awaited test results. Anxiety began to stake her claim. Everyone fiercely battled it while praying for another miracle. The test results revealed Angel's angel did not have the HIV virus, that she had been spared the horror many had anticipated. As one would imagine, Rachel unashamedly burst into tears while Angel clung to her for dear life.

"It's a miracle!" Ms. Tangy proclaimed, while Pastor Jim attempted to hide his tear-stained face.

"Yes it is!" Rachel gaily responded.

"They say men aren't supposed to cry."

"But our prayers have been answered, and the little one escaped that horrible disease. I can't help but cry. Tears of joy you know." Ms. Tangy and Pastor Jim's sob-filled conversation soon ended with a warm embrace. By then, everyone had gone into the nursery to get another glance of the newborn.

In the distance, Rachel heard the faint whisper of Angel. Though she was resting in the mother's ward, her voice was clearly distinct. "That's what we'll call her. We'll call her Miracle Diana Sutton." Ms. Rachel made her way to see the precious little one as Angel continued talking. "Ms. Rachel, I picked out her name last week, and Ms. Tangy looked up its meaning for me. She said she'd keep it a secret from you because I wanted it to be a surprise. She said her name means 'marvelous, heavenly, resident.'" Rachel turned to her right, as though she was in a dream, catching another glimpse of that sweet baby. The nurse then quietly placed the baby in her mother's arms. "Angel, you truly received a miracle." Rachel sighed in relief.

CHAPTER SIX

The Big Event

Six months had passed, and Miracle was blossoming quite nicely. Her tiny fingers and toes were filling out, and her dimples were making a name for themselves. Though Angel's breastfeeding career got cut short because of her HIV treatments, that didn't seem to slow our little Miracle down, not one bit. She was doing just fine and had quickly become Open Arm's darling. Everyone treated her like she was royalty, buying her the cutest things ever and making homemade nursery accessories in every color.

Her christening was just weeks away, and Pastor Jim and his Mrs. planned the whole thing. Reverend St. Clair was supposed to help Pastor Jim perform the ceremony while the children's choir prepared to ring their bells. A volunteer who was handy with a camera signed on as the official photographer, while a few teammates prettied up the dining room. Things were shaping up quite nicely, and all the employees and volunteers were invited to the festivities too. The Old Jamaican woman prepared a menu, which was the envy of them all. Everyone was ready to celebrate in grand style.

As Miracle's godmother, Rachel had the pleasure of dressing her for the occasion. Since the island didn't have the amenities of the mainland, her work was cut out for her. So Rachel called upon the skills of the island's best known seamstress and asked her to help out. They shopped and shopped for appropriate materials until they found the right fabrics. It took weeks to find, but finally they did. It was the most gorgeous lace ever seen. It was imported from Italy and cost a small fortune. But Rachel didn't seem to mind because that baby was special. She was their miracle.

Angel's treatment had been going well. She had rough days but was generally responding according to schedule. Her thick hair had begun to thin, becoming fine like that of a baby. Her pregnancy weight disappeared pretty quickly, but she didn't seem to mind. After all, she packed on an additional forty-five pounds while carrying Miracle. She had a glow about her; motherhood agreed with her in the most special way. She cared for her baby like a veteran mom of three though she wasn't. Angel handled her newborn like a pro. She knew how to nurse her newborn; she knew how to bathe her newborn, and she had motherly instincts when calming a fidgety Miracle. On that alone, no one ever feared Miracle would go out for adoption. Their mother-daughter bond was fiercely strong.

Since Rachel's own daughters had grown into beautiful young women with families of their own, they seldom saw each other because both their spouses were in the military, stationed in Germany to be exact. However, while Rachel was on the island, she corresponded with her brother, Terri, as much as possible. He knew all the latest gossip and always kept up to date with what was going on at church and in the community. He was busy as a marine reserve and Rachel as a missionary. There was little time for telephone conversations, plus it was so expensive that neither could afford it. So postcards and letters became their way of communicating. He'd heard all of her stories and was well aware of Rachel's love for Angel and her newborn. So she took a chance and invited her brother to Miracle's christening. She never expected him to agree, but he did.

The christening was just two weeks away, and things were heating up. The Old Jamaican woman was feeding the staff peanut butter and jelly while she busily prepared goodies for the event. Though Mr. and Mrs. Brown showed up to lend a helping hand, we knew she had bigger fish to fry, literally! The Browns were known to pop up at just the right time to do just the right thing. They were known for making contributions to the orphanage for years now and were such humble folks.

Time swiftly passed as everyone made preparations for the christening. The event was now two days away, and there just weren't enough hours in the day. Chores still had to be done. Chapel still needed to be attended and hospital rounds went on as though nothing else mattered. To add to that equation, Rachel's brother's flight was due within a few short hours. The anticipation was becoming more than one could bear. But it was all good. After all, Rachel hadn't seen her brother in just under a year. She missed him so and couldn't wait to see him again. He was the only family she had remaining, except her girls of course.

The airport was on the other side of the island, too far a drive for Rachel. She never took a liking to the dirt roads that twisted and turned a lot, plus if you weren't careful, you could slide off a cliff. So one of the volunteers agreed to take on that challenge, because they were natives and was familiar with the twists and turns the roads offered. Rachel was so relieved, and it was evident by her smile. She smiled and giggled all the way to the airport.

The reunion was worth the wait. They hugged, cried, and held on to each other like they did when they were children.

Rachel and Terri had always been close; the years nor the distance hadn't dampened it one bit.

Of course, one of the first things Rachel did was take Terri to meet Angel and Miracle. Angel had been released from the hospital and had moved in with Ms. Rachel. Because she was so young, the Children's and Families Society required her to live with Ms. Rachel until further arrangements could be decided upon. Rachel didn't mind at all. In fact, that was right up her alley.

Wouldn't you know, they hit it off like they'd known each other for years! Terri was captivated by Miracle and didn't want to let her go. He held her in his big burly arms and rocked her back and forth as if she were his own. Rachel was both shocked and amazed. *Who is this man holding Miracle? Could I being seeing some kind of hologram?* Rachel thought to herself. After all, her brother was notoriously fidgety around young children. *What happened to him? Whatever happened was very good because I like the new Terri*, Rachel commented with glee. They talked and talked until Miracle curled up on her side and cooed in her sleep.

Ms. Tangy, Terri, Pastor Jim, and Rachel later got together in the lounge to talk about the "good ole days." They laughed and talked about all kinds of stuff: good memories, funny memories, and precious memories. Volunteers kept popping in to see what was going on. After all, there hadn't been that kind of laughter going on for a few weeks now. Somewhere during the conversation, Pastor Jim slipped in a little something that knocked them off their feet. Seems a couple from Kingston Township showed interest in helping Angel out of her predicament. Word spread that Angel had given birth to a baby girl, that there might be a possibility she'd give her up for adoption. Since the couple had been unable to have a family of their own, having a baby would bring added joy to their lives.

Miracle could be the solution to their dilemma. Plus, they were people of means. They owned two grocery stores and some real estate. To that equation, their house was on the hillside, where the rich folks lived, and taking care of a newborn wouldn't be a problem. In fact, it seemed too perfect to be true! However, Rachel was devastated! She didn't want Angel to put Miracle up for adoption because in her mind, she belonged to everyone at Open Arms.

Finally, the time had come, and everyone was ready to celebrate. The tedious preparation showed signs of its success, as people made their way to the chapel. Filled to the brim it was, until an overflow tent had to be erected. To say the weather cooperated would be an understatement as the slight breeze off the ocean helped the typical island heat seem bearable. Open windows gave way to the sounds of the children's choir, providing an avenue through which their sweet sounds could be heard by the neighbors. Their tender rendition of "Jesus Loves the Little Children" brought everyone to a special place as their tear-stained cheeks voiced their personal testament of His love. Their bells rang in perfect harmony, and it was simply beautiful. Reverend St. Clair and Pastor Jim worked so well together. Each child knew their part and played their instrument to perfection. Rachel wore a dress she brought from back home. It had shades of soft peach chiffon with lace overlay, fitting her to a tee, then flaring outward. It was the perfect choice for the occasion, and everyone loved it.

"Rachel, I brought something for you to wear. I hope it's to your liking."

Rachel opened the small white box, and there lay a beautiful lavender orchid corsage. "Terri, your taste is impeccable. I love it."

"Thanks, sis."

"Would you please do the honors?"

"Of course, I would love to."

Rachel's glow was that of a doting mother. She had adored her brother her entire life, and now he was right there by her side. She could not have been happier.

There wasn't a dry eye in the house when Angel vowed to care for her child. Rachel was so proud of her inward strength and dignity. Her parents would have been beaming with pride too.

As Reverend St. Clair and Pastor Jim pronounced the blessing on Miracle, Mr. and Mrs. Brown stepped up to the microphone, making their intentions known publicly. The congregation was stunned.

"What did they say?" asked a surprised Ms. Tangy.

"I think they just offered to adopt our Miracle," Rachel reluctantly responded.

"Oh no. Dear Lord, please don't let that be the case," Ms. Tangy replied in disbelief. The congregation sat quietly as the mood suddenly shifted. It was a highly unusual thing to do. So Pastor Jim graciously thanked them for their intent and asked that they have a seat until the ceremony officially concluded. He was so diplomatic. No one was embarrassed but happy that he handled it all so well.

As they stepped outside the chapel, the celebration continued. Music could be heard everywhere. People were rejoicing, dancing, and congratulating Angel. She wore her million-dollar smile, and no one seemed to mind. It was a happy moment for her, and everyone wanted her to have that moment and then some.

Miracle grew weary of all the attention though and started fussing a bit. Surprisingly, Rachel's big brother stepped in. She melted into those muscular arms of his, and off to sleep she went.

Pastor Jim's wife helped out a lot, and everyone loved her for that. She played hostess to the hungry crowd and did so with such calm reserve. She was one of those "works behind the scenes" kind of wives, who could also be a most gracious hostess.

The meal was delicious. The old Jamaican woman made braised sirloin, stuffed baked potatoes, and green beans for the American side of the menu. Then there was the Jamaican side, which was filled with goodies like rice and peas, jerk chicken, curried goat, meat pies, carrot juice, and more. That day, no one was counting calories.

It had been a long but eventful day, and everyone was tired. However, Pastor Jim decided to meet with Mr. and Mrs. Brown about their intentions to adopt Miracle. They were a nice couple from Kingston Township, quite a ways from Rachel's tiny village. Polite they were, and certainly folks of means too. But there was something about them Pastor Jim couldn't quite put his finger on.

A few hours passed. With completed paperwork in hand and a huge donation to the orphanage, apparently the meeting was a success. Pastor Jim was gracious and thanked them as they went their way.

Meanwhile, Rachel's brother's visit was coming to an end. It had been such a brief trip, and she hated to see him go. They'd enjoyed a memorable reunion and had a ton of fun too. He was getting ready to leave when Pastor Jim called to say the couple had a sudden change of heart. They jumped for joy because none of them wanted their Miracle to be adopted. She was still part of the family, and again all seemed right with the world.

CHAPTER SEVEN

The Adoption

"Photo op everyone!" an ecstatic Rachel beckoned as the crowd gathered to watch the goings-on. Each pose revealed a tiny piece of Angel's harrowing story. From the twinkle in Angel's eyes to Ms. Tangy's stoic stance, the elements of uncertain drama could not go unnoticed. However, curled up on her mother's lap was baby Miracle; she was most definitely the center of attention. It was no secret; she was special, and everyone knew it, especially the Pastor Jim's Mrs. For this occasion, even she could not be found quietly hidden behind the scenes, but right up front by her husband's side, watching for the cameraman's cues all while displaying enough pride for them and everyone else. In their minds, you could hear them saying, "Our Angel survived." Most folks agreed there wasn't a finer moment ever on the island. Rachel stood to Angel's right along with her brother, Terri, and Ms. Tangy was there too. The cameraman took several poses just to be sure the essence of the day was adequately captured.

"The gown, make sure you catch the tiny train of her gown!" yelled Rachel as the cameraman planned each shot with precision and ease.

"I did. You"ll see it."

"Thank you," the two of them yelled back and forth to one another.

Folks were eating and talking and having a grand old time. However, in the back of Rachel's mind, curiosity lurked about, creeping in and out the crevasses attacking every emotion. "You know, the Browns might actually adopt our Miracle." she thought, and she didn't want the guests to catch a whiff of the inward struggle she was battling. So she quietly slipped away from the crowd of excited guests. There she noticed Pastor Jim standing over in the corner of the room. He wasn't talking to anyone either, just looking out the window with a blank stare on his face. *Strange*, she thought. So she walked up to him and said, "The ceremony was beautiful. You and Rev. St. Clair really connected. You did it perfectly. It was very touching."

"Thank you, Ms. Rachel. The ceremony was beautiful and that gown…What's the matter, you seem so quiet? What's on your mind?"

"Well, to be frank with you…the Browns. They seem so familiar, like I've dealt with them before."

"Really?"

"Yes, for some strange reason, I can't put my finger on it, but I know it will come to me sooner or later."

"By the way, that little Miracle just about stole everyone's heart today. Did you notice when I prayed for her, she smiled?"

"Yes, I noticed, Pastor Jim. She is a darling, a precious darling."

"And that Angel, she is so attentive. You'd never know she's just a child herself."

"She is pretty amazing, I must agree."

"Have you heard anything new from Angel's doctor?"

"No, seems she's responding to her treatments just fine. You know, there are side effects to be considered. But she doesn't seem to complain. Just takes it all in stride."

"Ain't that the truth," as their conversation ended with a giggle.

Just as Pastor Jim turned to walk away, he stopped midstream and yelled, "I know! I know!"

"What are you yelling about?" Rachel exclaimed.

"I know who the Browns are."

"Well, don't keep it from us now. Who are they?"

"When I arrived on the island, word around town was about a couple who lost all three of their children in a fire that destroyed their home. The parents weren't at home at the time. A babysitter had been hired to watch the children. After the children went to bed for the night, the babysitter fell asleep while smoking a cigarette. She woke up to fire and smoke engulfing the entire ground floor of the home, and she couldn't get to the children. By the time the fire department arrived, there wasn't anything they could do."

"Oh my, that is just horrible.

"I know. Since then, Mrs. Brown hasn't been the same, they say. Even worse, word around town is Mr. Brown sells drugs and has had trouble with the law. That's how he makes his money, how they've become so well off," explained Pastor Jim.

"Wow, that's some story. We can't let Miracle get caught up in that mess. I'm sorry, I know that's a strong word, but that's the best I can do right now."

"I know how you feel. But before we go making judgments, let's get some feedback from some other reliable sources."

"As usual, you're right, Pastor Jim. That's why you're the pastor and we're the volunteers!" Rachel giggled while walking away.

Now Angel had a quiet way about herself. She could slip in and out of a room without being noticed, and that she did well.

"Ms. Rachel, most of the guests have gone home, and I'm feeling a bit jaded. Would you mind watching Miracle for a few hours while I get caught up on some rest?" asked Angel.

"Are you kidding me? I'd love to watch Miracle. As a matter of fact, why not let her stay the night. I'd love to have her!"

"Thanks, Ms. Rachel. Here is her diaper bag. It is well-stocked. But if you need anything, you know where I'll be. Alright?"

"Sure, Angel. Go get some rest. Miracle and I will be just fine. Good night now."

"Good night, Ms. Rachel," Angel responded as she made her way out the door.

That had to have been one of the most memorable nights of Rachel's life. Thoughts of the early years flooded her mind, when her girls were colicky, teething, feverish babies. It all came rushing back as though it was just yesterday. And now, precious little Miracle and Rachel were getting to know each other. What an amazing time they had.

Rachel's favorite rocking chair was the perfect place to sing lullabies of yesteryear. Her tiny oval-shaped eyes stared back as if she understood Rachel's every word, and perhaps in her own way, she did. Needless to say, bath time was a hoot. Miracle screeched, cried, and splashed about just like any other baby. But the end result produced a sweet-smelling little one almost too precious for words.

The hours passed quickly, and morning arrived in the splendor and glory God intended it to. Within minutes, Rachel heard Angel's knock on the door. "Ms. Rachel, I came to get my baby girl. Did she give you any trouble? Did she cry a lot?"

"Calm down and stop with the questions. She's fine. We had a fine time last night. She was the perfect guest," Rachel replied.

"I'm so relieved, ma'am."

As Angel was refreshed from a good-night's rest, Rachel decided to approach her about "the adoption."

"Angel, do you know anything about the Browns, you know, the couple wanting to adopt Miracle?"

"No, ma'am. Folks around town have been chatting up about them for a while now, but I don't know what about. Why you ask, Ms. Rachel?"

"No reason, just curious," replied Rachel in the island accent that had grown on her.

"Well, I've got to be getting on. Got to get to class on time. I must hurry."

"Alright, we'll chat later, okay?"

"Yes, ma'am."

Angel hurried off to her classes as Rachel watched her dash down the path while basking in the memories of her special time with Miracle. As Pastor Jim walked down the hallway, he paused for a moment.

"Rachel, may I have a moment of your time?"

"Why sure, Pastor Jim. What is it?"

"I've spoken to the sheriff about the Browns."

"What did he have to say on the matter?"

"It was confirmed. Everything we discussed was true. As a matter of fact, I remember going to the prison and praying with Mr. Brown."

"What! You saw him in prison?"

"Yes, I didn't want to divulge that just yet, but the story is true."

"Oh my goodness, I can't imagine suffering something so horrific."

"Me neither. I pray that kind of heartache passes my doorstep."

"I know what you mean."

"Well, the sheriff doesn't recommend placing a child in that environment. He said Mrs. Brown hasn't been the same since the fire, and Mr. Brown has been caught dealing illegal drugs. We can't afford to place an infant in that situation. It wouldn't be the best thing to do. Perhaps that's why the Browns' had a sudden change of heart!"

"Well, that answers a few delicate questions I had in my mind. Pastor Jim, I want to adopt both Angel and Miracle so they can grow up together in the same home."

"Ms. Rachel, you are a remarkable woman. Open Arms is happy you came along. You've been a real blessing."

"Do you know how long it would take?"

"Normally, it's about a six-month period, but since you already know both mother and child, it might involve less time."

"Perhaps I'll talk to my brother about it."

Rachel returned to her room, thinking about her conversation with Pastor Jim and the possibility of adoption. "I suppose I should speak to Terri on the matter. Dear Lord, what's he gonna say?" The feeling of overwhelming fear struck Rachel's heart. After all, Terri and Rachel lived together in the old Victorian home that had been passed down to them, and Terri wasn't too fond of children but had warmed up quite nicely to Angel and Miracle. How was all that to work out. She tossed and turned, but could not fall asleep. So, Rachel decided to make a phone call.

"Hello, Terri, is that you?"

"Yes, this is me. Rachel, why are you calling at two thirty in the morning? What's going on?"

"I've been praying about something. I believe the Lord wants me to adopt Angel and Miracle."

"What? I think that would be a wonderful thing for you to do."

"You mean you don't mind?"

"No, of course not. When? How soon? I'll go ahead and contact a cleaning agency so they can tidy up the place before you come home. Just let me know when, okay?"

"Oh my goodness, Terri, I never expected you to say yes. I'm not sure when we'll actually leave the island, but you'll be the first to know, okay?"

"Okay," Terrie exclaimed.

"I love you."

"Ditto."

"We'll chat soon. I mean, I'll write and tell you about the particulars."

"Sounds good, Rachel. Now please, go back to sleep. I have to get up for work soon."

"Okay, good night."

Oh my goodness! Terri actually agreed and seemed happy about it. "Lord, thank you. Now please, help me to calm down and get some rest. In Jesus's name, amen. Rachel wasn't shy when it came to prayer, even when it was about getting some sleep!"

Dawn arrived wearing a huge smile and a blanket of colors beyond compare. In Rachel's mind, she'd already prepared her to-do list, and there was much to be done. So, she waltzed her way into the staff lounge bellowing, "Ms. Tangy, I have the most wonderful news!"

"Let me guess. You're going to adopt Angel and Miracle."

"How did you know?" Rachel happily responded.

"You know Pastor Jim can't keep a secret to save his life. He arrived at breakfast smiling like a Cheshire cat, and when I asked what made him so happy, he let the cat out of the bag."

"I should have known. Now I've got to find a good lawyer. Can you recommend someone, someone who is reputable yet affordable?"

"Sure. Try Attorney Ferdinand. He's got a decent reputation around town, and he practices family law."

"Alright, I'll check him out. Thanks, Ms. Tangy, and don't you go anywhere 'cause I might need your help again."

"Not to worry, you know where to find me."

"Thanks, Ms. Tangy, you're the best."

"Sure, Rachel, anytime."

Rachel's anxiety wouldn't allow her to sit still, not even for a moment. So she called him right away. "Attorney Ferdinand, my name is Rachel. I'm from the States, and I volunteer at Open Arms Orphanage. I'd like an appointment because I want to adopt two of the orphans, and I'd like to do it pretty quickly. When's your earliest appointment?"

"Well, Ms. Rachel. I think that's a wonderful thing for you to do. Let me check my calendar. Hmmm, there seems to be an available slot tomorrow morning at nine. Can you do that?"

"Yes, Attorney Ferdinand, I can."

"Okay, I'll see you then. Hold on one moment. My assistant will get your information."

"Thank you." Rachel's excitement was overwhelming, and her happiness hit a new peak.

Rachel grabbed her cell phone as quickly as she could. "Pastor Jim, I have some more good news!"

"What is it, Rachel?"

"I'm meeting my attorney tomorrow morning at nine."

"What? That's great! Let me know how things go, okay?"

"I'd be glad to," Rachel concluded.

Rachel's joy was so overwhelming she found it hard to contain, so she called her brother to share the news. "Hello, Terri, did I wake you again?"

"No, Rachel, I'm always awoke in the middle of the night waiting for my phone to ring. Of course, you woke me. I was trying to catch a nap," Terri growled in a less than friendly tone. "What's on your mind?"

"I found a wonderful lawyer who is willing to handle the adoption."

"That's great. What's his name?"

"His name is Attorney Ferdinand. Ms. Tangy recommended him."

"Well, that sounds like it could be a good thing."

With a deep breath and a heaping helping of hesitation, Rachel says, "Terri, word around town is adoptions are costly, and I might need your help. Can you?"

"Well, I don't know. I've spent a good bit of my savings on the renovations of Granny's place…our new home. But you already know that."

"Yes, I know."

"Well, what exactly will it cost, do you know?"

"They say about $7,000 each."

"How much are you going to need?"

"Are you sitting down?"

"Yelp." His voice takes a dip then slides into home base.

"About $7000…about half."

"I don't think I have that much in my savings, but I'll see what I can do. Don't worry, the Lord is on our side. He'll help us."

"Yes, Terri, I believe He will."

"Alright, sis, I love you, but sleep is calling my name."

"Alright, I love you too. Good night."

Time seemed to fly by as Rachel prepared for the meeting.

"Good morning, Attorney Ferdinand. My name is Rachel."

"Yes, we spoke yesterday. So you want to adopt two orphans from Open Arms?"

"Yes, sir. They're two very deserving children, and I'd love to have them as part of my family."

"Well, Ms. Rachel, you know they are both minors…Angel is without living parents, a ward of the Department of Orphans, Families, and Children and mother to a minor child…Hum. Is that right?"

"Yes, that's correct."

"Then it's a straight-forward case. However, the cost might add up a bit."

"Just how much are you talking about?"

"Each case could cost upwards $6000, plus fees of course."

"Well, I expected about that much, but I still want to move forward as soon as possible."

"Alright. Please get with my assistant. She'll let you know which documents you'll need to provide."

"Thank you, Mr. Ferdinand."

"My pleasure." They shook hands and walked away.

A few months passed since their meeting, and Rachel hadn't received any word from her attorney, and to that equation, the process appeared to be taking forever. But Terri had the nerves of steel; he was the perfect big brother, helping Rachel maintain a positive outlook. Pastor Jim, his Mrs. and Ms. Tangy prayed for her day and night, and she was glad they did because she needed it.

During the next few months, business went on as usual. The orphanage grew, chores went on, and everything was fine. Then after eight of the longest months of Rachel's life, the documents were finally ready to be signed, and the adoption was legalized.

Now Angel and Miracle had no idea what had occurred, and Rachel didn't want to bother them with the details. Ms. Tangy, Pastor Jim, and his Mrs. had quietly planned a celebration in Rachel's honor. She was such a diligent volunteer and hard worker, doing whatever was asked of her and most times more. So Ms. Tangy and Pastor Jim's Mrs. secretly booked a flight so Terri, her brother, could attend. Pastor Jim and his Mrs. had a knack for planning such things. The team came out in full force and gave her some of the nicest gifts you could think of. To add to that equation, that is when the announcement was made, that Angel and Miracle were officially part of Rachel's family. Needless to say, everyone was so happy, and having Terri by her side topped things off perfectly. It was wonderful.

Rachel's new family now consisted of four beautiful daughters, and she was thrilled.

CHAPTER EIGHT

Mission Possible

"Where has the time gone? Feels like I've been on the island an eternity!" Rachel exclaimed.

"I know. Just think, seems just yesterday Miracle was born, and now she's a walking, talking toddler getting into all kinds of trouble."

"Yes, Ms. Tangy, I know," said Rachel in her lighthearted tones.

So much had changed. The Open Arms Orphanage had grown, doubling its number of orphans and adding a new wing too. The Old Jamaican woman moved to the States, where she opened her own catering business, leaving everyone to fend for themselves. Though the interim pastor had done a fine job, Pastor Jim longed to get back to his own pulpit; he desperately needed to see about his congregation.

Angel, now high school age, was doing just fine. She had become quite good at sports. Angel was her name, and netball was her game. "Why don't you skip practice once in a while? Do you need to go every day?" Rachel exclaimed.

"It helps me stay fit," she replied. To that, Rachel had no argument or rebuttal. "Well, if sports makes you happy, then I'm happy too," a giggling Rachel replied. Lord knows Angel deserved a little happiness in her life. Besides, it gave Rachel a chance to spend time with Miracle. She was a growing, glowing toddler who loved getting into things. One day, Rachel heard a sloshing sound. So she called out to her, but Miracle didn't answer. Rachel searched and searched until she found her. Miracle was in the bathroom dunking her doll in the toilet. Can you imagine? "Miracle!" Rachel screamed in the stern tones most grandmothers hate to use. "That's not a good place to play!" The innocence of a child responded as she looked up with those oval-shaped eyes of hers and smiled as giggle juice dripped from her lips. What could Rachel say to that? Her innocence stole the show. So Rachel pulled the bathroom door closed so there wouldn't be a command performance! Off they went for a special bubble bath, doll included.

The next day was a special day because Angel had a game. She had been practicing and preparing for it for a while now, and excitement was in the air. Ms. Tangy and Rachel packed a light lunch, and with Miracle in tow, off to the game they went. It was an intensely close game. The Saints, the opposing team, was edging them out, and anticipation was at its peak. It was the Wind Jammer's turn, and Angel got into position. She took off with the speed of light, kicked the ball, and fell flat on her back screaming at the top of her lungs. Rachel immediately knew something had gone wrong, so she handed Miracle off to Ms. Tangy and ran out to the field. By the time she got there, Angel's coach beckoned the medical team to come and check on her.

Within minutes, Angel was hauled off the field, and the game went on without interruption. Her teammates went on to win the game by one point. It was a close one indeed. The crowd's cheers could be heard in the locker room. By the time Ms. Tangy arrived with the baby, Angel's team doctor gave the news they so feared. A broken ankle it was, and Angel would require further medical treatment. As usual, Rachel immediately went into mommy mode. "Dear Lord, please help her," she prayed. "Please protect her from further pain and harm."

The ambulance ride was swifter than Rachel had anticipated. After all, that was her first experience ever having to ride in one of those things. When they arrived at the hospital, the medical team took Angel in to see what was going on. "Seems she suffered a pretty ugly break…three distinct fractures. That could possibly require some surgery," said the physician while his hand rested on his hip and his head bobbed up and down. *How could such a serious injury happen? All she did was kick the ball,* was bouncing around in Rachel's mind. All she could think of was Angel's HIV status. How extensive would her surgery be? Would it require a blood transfusion? Was the blood bank well stocked? Just a whole lot of what ifs.

Within less than an hour, the doctor came back to speak with Rachel, confirming what she didn't want to hear. Angel's injury would require surgery. Rachel was amazed how quickly things moved along. Within a short period of time, Angel was prepped and wheeled into the operating room. So Rachel found a comfy spot where she sat and quietly prayed while she pretended to read a magazine. Fact is, the magazine was probably reading her. Anyway, the watchful eye of a nurse saw her in the quietness of that hour and came over to offer words of comfort. "Can I get you a cool drink or something to eat? It could be a few hours, depending on what the doctors find." Rachel's nerves went into overload, but she leaned on her faith. She had tons of practice doing that before, so now was no struggle at all. Somewhere in the back of her mind, she could hear Pastor Jim saying, "Whoever dwells in the shelter of the Most High will rest in the shadow of the Almighty" (Psalms 91:1) New International Version. She found strength in those words.

Three hours passed, and there had yet to be any word on Angel's condition. Though anxiety rose up searching for a place to dwell, there was always the presence of God's Word to calm her, pushing anxiety aside.

"Ms. Rachel?"

"Yes, sir."

"Angel did well. We were able to reset the breaks without any further damage to her ankle or loss of blood."

"Thank you, Jesus! I mean, thank you, sir." The young doctor giggled under his breath as if he understood the message she was trying to convey. The anticipation of the hour spoke loudly, and he knew Rachel was grateful things had gone well.

"If you'd like to see her, I'll have the nurse come and get you. Now remember, she's going to be a bit groggy, but she will be fine, okay?"

"Thank you so much for taking care of my Angel. She means the world to me," Rachel said in a quiet, reverent voice.

"I'm sure she does," the young doctor concluded.

Within minutes, Nurse Bonnie made her way down the hallway and escorted Rachel to Angel's room. There she was on her gurney. As Rachel stood by her bedside, she couldn't help but to say a prayer of thanksgiving. Angel had again pulled through a tough spot, and Rachel was more than happy about it.

"Angel, are you awake?"

"Yes, Ms. Rachel," she mumbled in her groggy, half-asleep voice. "I'm fine."

"Well, thank the good Lord. He looks out for us you know, and I'm glad He does. The doctor recommended you stay put for a few days so you can get some rest."

"Yes, ma'am. Where's Miracle?"

"She and Ms. Tangy went back to the orphanage. We didn't know how long you'd be, so they went on to get some supper. Did the doctor give you pain medication?"

"Yes, he said they would put me to sleep, but I'd feel better when I wake up."

"Well, you've got to get some food in your tummy before taking those pills you know, and hospital food isn't very appetizing. Ms. Tangy is making your favorite."

"You mean spaghetti?"

"Yes. That's been one of your favorite meals since you were a little girl."

"I can hardly wait."

"Oh, by the way, Ms. Tangy is going to help out with Miracle for a few days until you're feeling better."

"Thanks so much, Ms. Rachel. I really appreciate that."

"I know you do, sweetheart. I'll go now and get your supper. I won't be long. Until then, try to get some rest alright?"

"Yes, ma'am, I will."

During her hospital stay, Angel was a great patient. The staff loved her because she did whatever she was told to do. If they said, "It's time to go for a little walk," she would try her best to, even if it hurt a bit. Broken bones don't always heal quickly; however, Angel was the exception to that rule.

Within just three short weeks, Angel was hopping around without her crutches while Miracle tried desperately to mimic her. If ever there was a Kodak moment, that certainly was… simply priceless. The doctor said he had never seen anyone heal so quickly. But Rachel knew her Heavenly Father had been at work.

Pastor Jim had been planning his final revival for a while now, and the time had come. Choirs from different churches joined up as one big choir. They rehearsed and rehearsed, and by the sounds of it, their dedication paid off. Their numbers sounded like a bunch of Baptists belting away in harmony so tight and so well blended you would have thought they were Utah's own Mormon Tabernacle Choir. The ushers and greeters were all wearing their signature smiles and uniforms of black bottoms and white shirts so crisp and clean. Angel and her million-dollar smile was asked to join their group, and she happily obliged. With the help of her crutches, pointing folks in the right direction seemed the natural thing to do. After all, she'd spent hours decorating her crutches with scriptures and lots of bling too. They were a conversation all by themselves!

Pastor Jim had an anointing to fast like no one Rachel had ever known. He could fast days on end and not appear to be bothered by it. He taught the missions team scriptures on fasting, and they soon caught his vision and took part too. It produced such a glory on him. He was so filled to the brim with the Scriptures it was like watching a balloon ready to burst at first sight of a needle. Everyone knew he was in rare form, that the revival would be powerful because he spent time in His presence preparing.

The atmosphere was energy filled that first night, and anticipation was at maximum capacity as they eagerly witnessed firsthand what the Holy Spirit would do. The choir sounded like angels. "How Great Thou Art" became their signature song. Pastor Jim's Mrs. gave a warm welcome to all the guests in the attendance and introduced her husband as the night's preacher. He spoke from Jeremiah 29:11 and talked about being part of God's perfect plan. He told the crowd God's blessings would overtake them when they become obedient followers of Christ. His words were effective. You could see it on their faces as they held on to each word like they were gold. Soon, the altar was full; you could sense His Holy presence. Tears flowed, hearts were receptive, and souls were converted.

The next day, Pastor Jim felt he had completed his mission, tendered his resignation, gave his final speech to Open Arms's staff and volunteers, and spoke gaily about returning to the States. No one was happy about it because they didn't want that day to come. He had been such a blessing not just to Open Arms but the community as well. But he knew it was time for him to go home.

CHAPTER NINE

Getting To Know You, Settling In

The night quietly passed as everyone prepared for the flight home. Not only had the mission trip come to an end for Pastor Jim and his Mrs., but also for many others, including Rachel. Bags were packed and lined up on the tarmac while team members tearfully said their good-byes. It was now official; it was time to go home. The charter plane arrived on scheduled as planned while folks did some last-minute scurrying about.

It wasn't easy to say good-bye. Everyone had fallen in love with the islanders, and the islanders had fallen in love with them. Team members had worked hard and accomplished so much. New relationships had formed, and lifetime friendships to be remembered.

Angel was so excited. She had only dreamt of going to America. She was beside herself, giggling, singing, and showing off that million-dollar smile. Behind her smile though, her doe-like eyes gave rise to pangs of sadness. She was about to leave her home, teammates, classmates, and friends at Open Arms. Saying good-bye, for her, wasn't at all easy. But her pain was short-lived once she got a glance of the plane. Like most young people, her priorities quickly shifted, and fear took a backseat. Now, all she could talk about was getting on the plane! Miracle, however, was oblivious to all the commotion. She quietly sat in her swing, with tons of giggle juice on her chin, displaying her infant-like anticipation in the only way she knew.

"What time does the plane arrive?" asked Pastor Jim's Mrs.

"Ten o'clock is what's on the itinerary," Pastor Jim hurriedly replied. "We've got to get a move on!" His Mrs. hadn't taken the time to walk out to the tarmac. She did not know the plane was waiting for its passengers' arrival.

"I suppose I should call for help. Those bags look awful heavy, and I don't want you to injure yourself," said his Mrs.

"Thank you for thinking of that. I had totally forgotten just how tricky my back gets from time to time. You are the perfect wife, always so thoughtful."

"That's because I want you to be around when the grandkids finally come along," his Mrs. exclaimed.

"Let me give Rachel a quick call to see how things are going on her end. Alright?"

"Sounds like a plan to me!" said his Mrs. in her happy voice.

"Rachel, this is Pastor Jim. How are things going on your end?"

"We're just about ready. It's hard to believe the day has finally come. Seems we have been on this missions trip forever."

"I know. It's been two and a half years for me, but we are about to go home. I can't wait to see folks at church."

"Yes, I can't either. Well, let me light a fire under Angel. She moves kind of slow sometimes. But, I'll see you in a few minutes," Rachel responded. "Okay, until then," said Pastor Jim as he quickly moved on.

Rachel, with her list in hand, tried desperately to think of everything her Angel and Miracle might need. Lightheartedly, she asked, "Angel, about the diaper bag, are there extra clothes for Miracle?"

"Yes, Ms. Rachel. I also packed snacks and two bottles."

"Alright, seems we're about ready to go."

"Yeah! I'm so happy, Ms. Rachel. I can't wait to give Uncle Terri a hug. He'll be waiting at the airport, won't he?"

"Yes, of course he will," she said with a slight smile in her voice. "Oh, I almost forgot, Angel, did you pack your medications?"

"Thank you, Ms. Rachel. I'd forgotten about them. There's so much on my mind these days."

"I know, Angel."

An hour passed, and the sound of golf carts could be heard racing around. Filled to capacity with team members, luggage, and smiles from ear to ear, everyone was on their way to board the flight.

"Let's gather for a moment of prayer and thanksgiving," Pastor Jim proclaimed. "Amen, amen" could be heard throughout the crowd, as they bowed their heads in reverence. "Dear Heavenly Father, thank you for giving us such an opportunity to bless the orphans and islanders. We ask that you continue to shine your love upon them. Grant them protection and supernatural provision. Allow them to know they are loved no matter what. In Jesus's name we pray, amen." As the crowd disbursed, Rachel heard Pastor Jim say, "Look, that gentleman is wearing a uniform. He must be our pilot."

Out from behind the plane stepped a muscular good-looking young man. "Good morning, family. My name is George, and I'll be piloting your flight today. We'll be cruising at 32,000 feet altitude. Nothing to worry 'bout. Just sit back, buckle your seat belts, and enjoy the ride." His pristine island accent flowed effortlessly from his lips. Rachel turned to her right, catching a glimpse of a nearly comatose Angel. It was worth all the coins in her pocket because Angel was almost catatonic! After all, the pilot was a tall, slender, handsome man whose smooth mocha complexion could put a lump in any young woman's throat, and Angel was no different. She couldn't keep her eyes off of him.

Lightheartedly, Rachel asked, "Angel, are you okay?" giggling as the words slid off her lips.

"Yeah, why are you asking?"

"Uh, nothing. Well, actually you were staring at the pilot."

"Was I?"

"You were! But, that's alright," Rachel chuckled.

"I'm sorry, Ms. Rachel, but he's quite the catch. He's *fine*!"

"What does that mean?" as if she didn't know.

"That means he's an attractive man. I bet he's much older than me though," Angel said in a disappointment-filled tone.

"Maybe not, the only way you'll find out is by talking to him. Just general talk now. Let him do most of the talking, you hear?"

"Yes, ma'am. I guess you're right. But I don't think I have the nerve to ask him any questions. I would just faint!"

"You young people are so funny. Wait a bit, and then get a conversation going. You might actually get lucky," proclaimed Rachel with a slight smile in her voice. "Look, there's Pastor Jim and his Mrs.," said Angel, trying to change the conversation to something other than the pilot and his good looks.

"Boarding flight 227 at gate 9, flight 227 at gate 9," the announcer bellowed over the intercom.

"That's us, Angel!" They quickly scurried their way to the gate and boarded the flight. Within minutes, they were airborne and on their way home. Just moments into their flight, the flight attendants got a glance of Miracle and immediately took a liking to her. She was such the well-behaved little traveler. Babies don't particularly like changing altitudes, and some adults don't either. But Miracle never cried, not once. She lay in Angel's arms nibbling on her snacks with the contentedness of an old pro. But Rachel's mind was on something else.

"Have you talked to George yet?"

"Who's George?"

"The pilot! You mean to tell me you've forgotten about him?"

"Yes, I did. That's because I'm not gonna be asking some man a bunch of questions about his personal life. Anyway, he's been busy, and I don't think passengers are allowed in the cockpit, are they?" Angel asked with a hint of hope.

"Of course not, but if he walks down the aisle, I'm gonna grab him," exclaimed Rachel.

"Dear Jesus, please let him stay where he is! Please don't embarrass me, Ms. Rachel," a voice penetrated Angel's thoughts.

"Alright, I know what you are thinking, and I won't embarrass you," Rachel reluctantly agreed.

Four hours and thirty minutes later, Rachel and Angel stepped off the plane with Miracle in tow. Just as promised, Terri was waiting at the gate. You could see him a mile away. With arms stretched high was a bright colorful "Welcome Home" banner and plenty of balloons too. It was a happy day!

The ride from the airport was filled with conversation. Everyone was talking over everyone else; each trying to get a word in edgewise. It sounded like a football team, meeting in a huddle, discussing their next play. Each had something to say and wouldn't stop until their voice had been heard.

Once they arrived, getting settled in was no difficult task. Terri made certain everyone would be comfortable. Rachel hadn't ever seen Terri so happy before. If Miracle wasn't on his lap, she was in his arms. Angel, on the other hand, couldn't fit in his arms, but she had certainly stolen a huge chunk of his heart. While Rachel was away, her brother hired an architect to draft plans for a new addition just for Angel and Miracle. Rachel couldn't imagine him being so generous; he'd never been that way before. He was like a new man, and Rachel liked that a lot.

Their first meal together was simply hilarious. That's when they discovered Miracle prefers wearing her mashed potatoes. Sweet peas and mashed potatoes were on the menu, and they went everywhere—on the wall, the carpet, and on her. But she didn't seem to mind at all. Guess it's because she didn't have to be part of the cleanup crew. Her Uncle Terri did the honors and enjoyed every minute of it. He wore his camera constantly; it was attached to his hip like a piece of vital equipment. He captured snapshots of just about everything anyone did, especially the funny moments. You never knew when you would be caught doing something silly.

The weekend arrived, and it was time to go to church. The eleven-o'clock service was everyone's choice simply because it gave them more time to get ready, and more people attended that service too. As there were plenty of hugs to give out, that service would definitely allow them the chance to get the task accomplished. Pastor Jim got up and thanked everyone for their prayers during his absence, complimented the itinerant pastor on doing a fine job, and gave his Mrs. a big smack on the cheek just because he was so happy to be home. The congregation welcomed Rachel, Angel, and Miracle with a rousing applause and loved on them like they were old timers. The day had been filled with joy and laughter, and now the recliner was calling Rachel's name.

As Rachel reflected on the events of the day, she became overwhelmed with joy. Reflecting on the Bible story of Jacob and Rachel to be exact (Genesis 29:1–14), she somehow felt connected to the story. The Bible story mentions how Rachel suffered the embarrassment of losing her beloved Jacob to her sister Leah, that it had become an overcrowded love story where Rachel had no voice. She longed for happiness with Jacob, but Leah was enjoying her moment. Soon, however, God's purposes would be revealed, and Rachel began to live out the true meaning of who she was, a "ewe," the symbol of prosperity and security. As the story goes, Rachel and Jacob were finally wed after many years of hard work. They had a son who they named Joseph. He later became a ruler, a man of great wealth and substance during the time of famine and was able to provide not just for himself, his wife, and children, but for his brothers and their families as well. Those were the same brothers who threw him into a pit and sold him into slavery. But by God's grace, Joseph survived. Even better than that, before Jacob, Joseph's father, closed his eyes in death, he witnessed the prosperity and security that Rachel had given birth to. The prophetic significance of her name had come full circle.

Though Rachel had read that Bible story many times before, she could identify with every part of it not because they shared the same name, but because both had suffered betrayal, loss, and the need to live purposefully. The emotion, strong and unrelenting, washed over her like fresh rain. Again, she was vulnerable, wanting to please the Lord. She could sense a rebirth of some kind, but what exactly she didn't know. To that point, Rachel felt her life had been on hold, her purpose resting as if it were a precious gem hiding in a seasoned piece of cheesecloth, a place of quietness. Though she enjoyed that season, she knew it wouldn't last forever.

Somehow, in the days ahead, during the stillness of the evening hours while Angel and Miracle were asleep, pieces of Rachel's destiny found each other and joined together like a puzzle. She dusted off those pieces, gathered what was left of herself, and asked her Heavenly Father for guidance. Soon, it became clear what she was to do.

Among those pieces of Rachel's destiny lay a large chunk of the puzzle covered in dust. On it the words "Raise up lost, lonely, and hurting women" were inscribed. The pain of her past now began to take on new meaning. Just like Rachel of the Bible, her life was now symbolic. It had purpose, which included the futures of two precious orphans, Angel and Miracle. If you've ever read the book of Genesis, you'll see how their son Joseph became a great ruler and a prosperous man who provided financial security to his entire family during the time famine. Now, you must know famines are not just a shortage of food, but manifest themselves in other ways, such as emotions, love, finances, health, and so much more. God healed her heart; the devastation of Rachel's past no longer held her captive, because her "famine" was now ended.

CHAPTER TEN

Full Circle

Pastor Jim's Mrs. headed up the Women's Ministry at their church, and each year, she would plan an annual retreat for the ladies. That's when she would invite guest speakers to come in and speak to the women on how they should live purposeful lives, as well as fun stuff too. His Mrs. had a knack for finding special spots perfect for those types of events, and this year was no exception.

There was an old convent about thirty-five miles to their east; it sat on the coastline with views that would take your breath away. To that equation, it had the most darling retreat facility ever. So one weekend, the nuns invited the group to come down and experience it for themselves. Typically, the nuns would rent it out as a way of building revenue for their school. His Mrs. didn't mind helping out and did not hesitate to oblige, not one bit. Along with her, she took a small group of ladies from the congregation to get some much-needed quiet time. Well, the most wonderful thing happened when they put their heads together. They came up with the idea of sponsoring a trip to Niagara Falls, the Canadian side, just for the ladies!

Well, when the announcement was read at church the following Sunday, thunderous applause nearly drowned out the poor announcement clerk. It was as if clouds bumped into each other and suddenly burst into rain. Tears of joy flowed, and the deal was sealed. Going to Niagara Falls they were! When Pastor Jim's Mrs. asked, "Are ya'll wanting to go with us?" Rachel, along with many other women, quickly responded with a resounding yes.

Months quickly passed and there was little time left to prepare for the trip. So Rachel decided she would cook a few meals and put them away in the deep freezer for Angel and Terri so that chore they wouldn't need to worry about. They didn't seem to mind, not one bit.

The day approached, and the women were buzzing about like busy bees. The anticipation was so thick you could cut it with a knife. "Am I the only light-packing woman among the group?" Rachel asked as dozens of suitcases and carry-ons were lined up next to the bus. Red ones, blue ones, grey ones, multicolored ones all waiting to be hoisted into the luggage bay.

"Mrs., do you need my help? That bag looks awfully heavy."

"No, Rachel, I"ll be fine. I've built up a few muscles over the years," she giggled. "Housewifing works wonders you know. Best exercise I ever got was when I was doing chores." "Yes, Mrs., I know," replied Rachel as she boarded the bus.

Now, the bus ride was the best ever. They laughed, played silly games, and reminisced about days gone by when they had thicker hair and trimmer waistlines.

Rachel liked doing the tourist thing. She took snapshots of just about every site possible, including many other tourists. From her hotel suite, the view was simply glorious. From the falls to the county fair, there was so much to take in. The falls were breathtaking, and the fair drew quite a crowd. So

Rachel decided to go for a walk and check things out. The place was packed like a can of sardines. It became obvious his Mrs. alone wasn't the only person whose thoughts were on the falls, there were tourists everywhere. No one was disappointed by its beauty. It was all that Rachel had expected and then some.

Have you ever been to an amusement park? I'm sure you have. They're filled with exciting rides and fun things to do, and the hotdogs and cotton candy are the best!

From Rachel's youth, she held on to her memories of fun times she had at amusement parks, She loved the Ferris wheel too. It had always been her favorite ride. She didn't know if it was the screams of joy and terror that was so captivating or dangling on a Ferris wheel midair with the possibility of falling to one's death that brought on a thrill like no other. But somehow she was hooked. So Rachel decided to take a spin for old time's sake, and she nearly lost her lunch! That's when she decided it was time to retire from that thrill.

As she got off the Ferris wheel though and walked away, she took a quick glance back at that wheel circling around and around. It reminded her of herself and how her life had been great but that her divorce alone possessed the power to alter her life's course. It had haunted her before. She could never predict its onset, but when the memories hit, they attached feelings of disdain and unpleasantness.

For instance, once Rachel's divorce was finalized, she tried desperately to get settled in Grandma's old place. For her, it meant the end of one season and the beginning of something new. She was passionate about moving on. While Terri was out of the country and not readily available to help with the hands on stuff, bumps in the road came out of nowhere. The carpenter complained about the electrician. The electrician complained about the plumber, and on and on they went. Each seemed to want a pound of her flesh, or so she felt. She soon learned that pulling permits and negotiating with contractors could take on a life of its own, one that she wasn't too fond of.

While contractors were completing updates on Grandma's house, she ended up storing her things and moving into a hostel. That was the best she could do and what she could afford at the time. It was certainly not part of her plan. She was very uncomfortable and not fond of sharing her space with total strangers. But she managed to get by. Her choices were few; she had to. She had already tried living out of her car and bunking in at local shelters, but the concern for her safety soon became an issue. She had things stolen out of her room, money disappeared from her purse, and no one would come clean about who had done the dirty deeds. Finally, law enforcement came to her rescue, and missing things began to resurface. That brief time of quietness and peace did not last very long because soon other unpleasant episodes erupted.

The contractor's less than ethical behavior became an issue, vexing poor Rachel to no end. The completion of Grandma's old house got pushed further and further back while living at the hostel got more and more uncomfortable. As deadlines approached, fear and anxiety somehow crept in and found a temporary place to dwell. Rachel's stress level got maxed out like a credit card. But she tried her best to hold it together, only ending up emotionally and physically drained. She developed some kind of virus and couldn't keep any foods down. Gatorade and Pepto-Bismol were the main courses on her menu for days. After several trips to the emergency room and an overnight stay that pushed her to the edge, she felt overwhelmed; she had, had her fill. "Dear God, how much more? I don't know who I am anymore. I don't know what happened or where things got off course. But I humbly ask your forgiveness, for help and guidance," became Rachel's prayer plea. Within a few short days, things began to get better. She was able to keep foods down without the assistance of the pink stuff, her strength was creeping back to its normal place, and a friend stepped in to assist with the remodeling project.

When Rachel was finally released from the hospital, she made a trip to the local library; it was just around the corner from the hostel, and she felt up to the task. She loved to read romance novels among other things. She heard of a new novelist and ordered a few of her books, which arrived and needed to be picked up to. As a regular patron, she knew how the books were categorized and shelved. However, as she walked the aisles, she was drawn to the inspirational section where the Bible help materials were stored. As part of who Rachel was, she never did anything without first asking the Lord's guidance, and this time wasn't any different. Almost immediately, her attention was drawn to a book titled *Put Your Past Behind You and Focus on Your Future* by Timothy Johns of From My Heart to Yours Family Ministries. She took a moment to peruse and gleaned what she could. As she placed the book back on the shelf, Rachel immediately knew there was something else, something more. Other books grabbed her attention, all authored by some of our nation's finest Bible teachers. His presence could be sensed, and Rachel felt an inner peace and decided to check them out. While standing in the aisle, she read and feasted on their words like a hungry child. Rachel knew she was hearing from God and began writing down scriptures, reading its words while examining her heart. What was soon discovered saddened her greatly. Like David, her joy was gone. Somewhere along the way, Rachel had become burdened with cares, negative emotions, and ungodly behaviors. She began blaming it all on the temper she inherited from her father. Though that was not the culprit, and it may have been a contributing factor; the problem was sin. She had to call it for what it was. It manifested itself in anger and depression and short-temperedness. Those are works of the flesh, not works of the Spirit (Galatians 5). Rachel knew God wasn't pleased.

As she walked back to the hostel, she knew her task now became very important. She needed to stop using her weaknesses as rebellion against her destiny because Gods purposes for Rachel were yet to be fulfilled.

That is what the Ferris wheel recanted to her, that God's purposes for her were yet to be fulfilled. She now began to recognize the pain buried deep within was a byproduct of her past, its purpose to help propel her into her future, that her obedience to God resulted in her new connection with Angel and Miracle, and finally, that their place in her life meant more than she had imagined. A sense of excitement overcame Rachel; she knew something good was on the way.

For the remainder of her time at the Niagara Falls, Rachel felt uplifted knowing God had something wonderful in store for her. She rushed back to her suite, where she immediately fell to her knees and repented for ever doubting Him, asking that He "wash me thoroughly from my iniquity" (Psalms 51:2) King James Version. Then she took a long deep breath and exhaled a sigh of relief.

It's amazing what happens when we carry the messes of yesterday into our tomorrows. That's what Rachel was doing. She had forgiven the folks who had hurt and disappointed her. But she doubted anything good would come of her life, quietly rehearsing the offense of her past over and over again when she simply needed to let them become history.

After all, God had blessed her with two new extended family members, Angel and Miracle. Everything she lost in her divorce was now restored. She had the love and support of her brother Terri, Grandma's old Victorian home, and the fresh memories of her extended family all within arm's reach.

Rachel's life had come full circle.

CHAPTER ELEVEN

The Call

Several years had quickly passed. Rachel's room was thriving, Angel was all grown up, and Miracle was a fifth grader at Wild Oates Elementary School. Terri, now retired, spent his every waking moment down at the reserve office talking to new recruits. They had finally found their places, destinies, and callings both as individuals and as a family. It was great. God had truly smiled on them, and they were pleased. Who would have known Rachel would have survived the devastation of her past, be called of God, and made useful for His glory? But that's what God did! It was simply wonderful. Her pain had found a resting place in the arms of her savior, right where it belonged. She no longer carried its burden, and she was one happy gal. The memory of it seemed distant and far away; no longer any emotion tied to it. God had done a work in her heart that only He could accomplish, and she rejoiced.

Rachel's Room was the spiritual baby she gave birth to. It had quietly been hiding in the crevices of her mind for years now. It was a place of healing, transitional housing for women who experienced similar pangs of unpleasantness. Her rooms were filled with women from every background: uneducated women, college-educated women, single moms, women of no means, and even ex-cons. Their commonality was an ache, a pain, and a desire for a better life. They wore the battle scars of painful pasts and had become part of a delicate club known as "survivors." It was only by His grace that many of them weren't destroyed by their circumstances. Most of their lives had been filled to the brim with abuse; sexual, emotional, physical, and mental abuse had marred their memories for life. Though each had a story to tell that was often difficult to listen to, that never deterred Rachel from extending open arms and a listening ear. To her, they were her babies, and all she wanted for them was a better life.

As time quietly passed, Rachel's Room gained quite the reputation. Rachel wasn't the type to crave attention from folks in town. Low key she was, often sitting in the shadows of her "babies" as they walked the path of healing and wholeness. Some through twelve-step programs, others through counseling, then there were those who found a peace that can only be found in Jesus Christ. It became obvious; His hand was definitely upon their lives, changing them from the inside out.

Rachel's Room was her favorite place to be aside from church. She loved being there, talking to and loving on her "babies." It was therapeutic. Each time, she hugged someone, flashed a smile, or reassured someone that tomorrow would bring new mercies and untapped opportunities; it was like she was talking to herself. Only an amazing Heavenly Father could have orchestrated that.

Now, Angel loved working with the women, and because she was so good at it, Rachel made her an assistant. Her passion was evident, so Rachel taught her everything she knew. She was the best assistant ever, and the women loved her. She was down to earth and could easily relate to them and their situations. Most importantly, she understood the need for confidentiality. After all, Angel had quite the past too!

Pastor Jim heard how nicely she'd been doing over at the Room and decided to check things out for himself. So one sunny Saturday afternoon, Pastor Jim put his chores aside and took his Mrs. for a little spin. It was a nice day for that kind of thing. Blue skies mixed with puffy clouds were the weatherman's prediction, and that day, he was right. On the way there, Pastor Jim and his Mrs. reminisced about how things used to be while making googly eyes at each other. Hard to believe, after so many years, those two were still in love. Like a couple of teenagers they were. An hour had swiftly fled, and they hadn't realized it until they pulled into the quiet cul-de-sac where Rachel's Room hid among the most beautiful white oaks.

Their welcome was as warm as usual. Lots of hugs and kisses were definitely on the agenda.

"Rachel, has Angel ever mentioned going to Bible college or seminary?" asked Pastor Jim.

"No, she never said anything about it to me. If she ever does, I will let you know. Why do you ask?" Rachel inquisitively responded.

"Well, I believe Angel might be just the person to carry on in your absence. She certainly has what I call leadership tendencies. She's caring, compassionate, and so much more."

"Who has what it takes?" Angel yelled as she burst through the door of Rachel's office.

"Angel, is that you?"

"Yes, Ms. Rachel, it's me."

"Well, yes. Pastor Jim and I were discussing you. Can you please come and sit for a minute? We'd like to ask you something."

"Alright." Angel came in and found a comfy spot to rest. "What's your question?"

"Well, we've been hearing some nice things about you. The women at the Room seem to like you a lot, and you're always volunteering at church. So we thought you might want to go away to Bible college. We think you'd make a fine director one day."

"*Me?*"

"Yes, you!" Rachel replied.

Their voices penetrated her thoughts as she stood frozen in time, and with sheer disbelief written all over her face, Angel bellowed, "I'd love to! When I was a little girl on the island, I wanted to be a missionary. For me, this is like a dream come true," replied an ecstatic Angel as tears flowed from her big beautiful eyes.

"Well, seems we've got a bit of work to do…some ground to cover. Pastor Jim and I will get some things in order," replied a more-than-pleased Rachel.

"I've known from the day that girl set foot on the grounds of Open Door that she was special. I couldn't be more pleased," exclaimed Pastor Jim.

"I know. I can't wait to see what happens next," an excited Rachel responded.

The coming weeks seemed to fly by. Everyone was busy doing what they do best. Pastor Jim preached like a man from another world, Terri was busy hauling in new recruits by the dozens, Miracle was becoming a straight-A student, and Rachel was nursing on her patients while handing out hugs and kisses by the dozens. With the duties of their day under their belts, Rachel, Pastor Jim, Angel, and Miracle settled down for some kitchen table talk.

"Ms. Rachel, there's a ton of mail on the table. I brought it in from the mailbox."

"Thanks, Angel."

Angel quietly observed her fifth grader. "Miracle, how is your homework coming along?"

"I'm good, Momma. Needn't worry none."

"I'd still like to check it out."

"Okay, Momma. I should be done soon," Miracle replied.

Out of nowhere Rachel's alarm-filled voice could be heard. "Angel, Miracle, come quickly!"

"What's the matter?"

"An envelope came from the Bible College. It's addressed to you, Angel. Open it. Hurry!"

"Alright, Ms. Rachel."

"I'm sorry, Angel. I get excited sometimes. Please hurry. I can hardly contain myself."

"That's alright, ma'am," Angel responded.

A quietness swept over the room as anticipation stood tall and wide. Finally, a slight reaction emerged as a weird smirk shadowed Angel's face, resting on her cheeks like a cloud. By then, Rachel's face went gray, and for a moment, it was as though she had stopped breathing. "Oh no, she didn't get in," Rachel cried as a tiny tear gathered in the corner of her left eye. She began scurrying about like a mother hen. "Something must have gone wrong. I'll call Pastor Jim, and we'll make a few phone calls," she said with her hanky in hand. "Got to find out what happened. It'll be alright. It'll be alright," she kept repeating. By then, Miracle noticed Rachel's dissatisfaction and quickly reacted by putting her arms around Rachel's waist. She offered the kind of reassurance that only she could. It was child-like; it was innocent.

"Ms. Rachel, is everything okay?"

Rachel quickly gathered herself as she felt the young girl's pangs of fear. "Of course, sweetheart. It"ll be okay."

"Well, I don't know what the fuss is about," bellowed Angel. "I got accepted into their internship program."

"What?" yelled Rachel. Laughter burst forth like leaky water kegs washing away the tension that had so quickly built itself a place to dwell. Everyone rejoiced, including Pastor Jim, who was in on it the whole while. "What else does the letter say?" asked Rachel as she giggled aloud. "I have to go back to the island for three months. Open Arms requested I intern there."

"Back to the island! What about Miracle? Are you taking her too?" screamed a concerned Rachel. By then, she had ridden the rollercoaster of disappointment, elation, and now shock.

"It's during the summer, Ms. Rachel. Miracle can come along. She'd love to find out what it's like to live on the island, to know where her momma came from. Wouldn't you, Miracle?"

"Yes, ma'am. Please, Ms. Rachel, say I can go." Refusing those round doe-like eyes was never an easy task for Rachel, and she didn't have the heart to say no.

"Alright, Miracle, but just for the summer," Rachel concluded. Shouts of joy could be heard throughout the house, and Pastor Jim rejoiced by doling out a few hugs and kisses along the way. It was a happy moment.

"Hi, everybody. What's all the fuss about?" asked a confused Terri.

"I got accepted to Bible college. Open Arms wants me to do my summer internship there. Isn"t that something?"

"Open Arms...on the island? Is that what you're talking about?"

"Yes, Uncle Terri. Ms. Rachel said I could go too!" an excited Miracle chimed in. Well, that bit of news burst Terri's bubble! He was not smiling, no not at all.

"Rachel, have you lost your mind? That child cannot miss school. She can't go, and that's final."

"Terri, it's just for the summer. She'll be out of school. It will be a great opportunity for her to see where her momma comes from."

"I don't like the idea of Miracle going so far away, but"—silence took a semi-permanent place in the room—"I guess it will be alright. Just this one time," Terri said begrudgingly. Angel and Miracle both recognized the sternness of his tone but quickly tackled him with huge hugs and lots of gratitude.

"Well, looks like it's a rap!" Pastor Jim surmised.

"Are you coming on the trip with us?"

"Yes, I'll be traveling to the island too. Since it's such a short trip, plus the Mrs. says I can. Can't do that if she doesn't give permission you know," he said with a slight giggle in his voice.

"Good," Angel replied. "Momma, when do we leave?" asked an anxious Miracle.

"Next week," Angel replied.

"Yeah, I'm so happy!" yelled Miracle.

Packing for the trip wasn't the easiest task. Rachel and Terri made lists that grew more and more each day.

"All that stuff will not fit in this suitcase," Angel proclaimed.

"It has to. You need every bit of it," Rachel and Uncle Terri both replied in one voice. "And don't forget your meds!"

"Alright, I won't. I suppose you know what you're doing 'cause you've done this before. I can hardly believe the trip is just a few days away. I'm so happy," said Angel as excitement oozed out in her voice.

The flight was a quick one, and before you knew it, the internship had begun. The first week seemed a bit tedious. Miracle had no memory of life on the island. She had become so Americanized it was just too funny!

"Momma, the bathrooms are outside!"

"Yes, what did you expect? Just put on plenty of bug spray...you know the stuff in the blue and orange can. Uncle Terri put in your suitcase. You"ll be alright."

"Yuck," Miracle replied, dragging every word to the ground with hints of disapproval.

Two months passed swiftly, and they had become more than acclimated to the ways of the island. Miracle pitched in wherever she was needed, and Pastor Jim made good use of Angel's skills. She had a way with words, just like Rachel. She could put them together and let them out all at the right time. People loved listening to her speak, and Pastor Jim knew it all too well. "Angel, we're having chapel tomorrow afternoon. Can you speak a few words to the people?"

"Who, me? I'm not a preacher."

"I know, but you're so much like your ma, Rachel. I think the Lord wants you to speak tomorrow. Can you?"

"Well, I do have a testimony. You know about my illness and how God has helped me."

"Yes, I think the people would love to hear about that."

"Alright," Angel agreed.

Later that evening, Pastor Jim, so elated at what took place during chapel, was compelled to make a call to the States. "Rachel, I wish you were here to see it for yourself."

"It's three o'clock in the morning. What are you talking about?"

"Angel spoke at chapel earlier today, and she lit the place up! It was like revival!"

"What?"

"She talked about her illness and how God gave her a miracle, literally. She talked about how He helped her feel better, and she talked about you and Terri, how nice y'all have been to her and Miracle. She sounded so much like you till it was almost unbelievable! But the best part is, the altar filled up, and people were giving their hearts to the Lord Jesus Christ. The team must have counted about 150 people or more. I'm so excited till I can't hardly contain myself."

"Pastor Jim, that is such good news. I knew she had it in her. I told her that when she was just a child."

"You know God is good, and He's merciful."

"Yes, Pastor Jim. He is."

"Well, I've got to go now, Rachel. It was good talking to you. Oh, and please don't let on to Angel that you know how well she did. Okay?"

"Okay," Rachel concluded.

Meanwhile, the internship kept Angel so busy until she hadn't realized the summer had quietly slipped away.

"I don't know where the time went, Miracle. We'll be flying home in two weeks. Have you enjoyed yourself since you've been here?" asked Angel.

"Yes, ma'am, I have," Miracle replied.

"Pastor Jim asked that I visit the orphans this afternoon. While I'm busy with them, you can go down to the playground if you like."

"Can I, Momma?"

"Yes, you may. I shouldn't be too long. Be careful now, and behave."

"Yes, Momma."

While Angel prepared herself to see the orphans, a strange feeling came over her. *I dislike feeling this way. There must be a hundred butterflies buzzing around in my stomach right now. I only get this feeling when something is about to happen. I wonder what it could be. Oh well, time to get on my way*, Angel thought to herself as unanswered questions penetrated her mind.

Ms. Rachel taught me how to clock this path when I was a child. I wonder if I can do it as quickly now. Let's give it a try. Angel picked up speed as she walked the cobblestoned path.

"I'm not going to make it. I must hurry!" Angel thought out loud. "Oh no, my shoe just came untied." Just as she bent down to fix it, she bumped into a tall very handsome man. "I'm so sorry, sir. I was just trying to fix my shoe lace."

"Not to worry, ma'am. It's alright. Here, let me help you. Sit and rest for a moment," said the stranger in the smoothest tones Angel had ever heard.

"Sir, what is your name? If I don't thank you properly, my momma Rachel will have my head on a platter!"

He responded with a giggle. "My name is George."

"George?" Angel confirms.

"Yes, ma'am, my name is George."

Well, by this time, Angel's mind was racing. *No, it couldn't be the pilot from years gone.* Trying her best not to become noticed, she looked again to be sure it wasn't him. His well-groomed mixed gray hair, facial features, and pressed professional look all confirmed her fears. "Dear God, it is him!"

CHAPTER TWELVE

Simply Smitten

"My name is George, and I'm a pilot with Island Airlines. Been doing the same job for a few years now, 'cause I love flying. It's so peaceful up there. What about you?"

Still shocked that she would ever run into that pilot again, Angel quietly gathered herself. "I'm Angel, a missionary from the States."

"That's a good thing, ya know."

"Thank you. I was orphaned when Hurricane Diana hit the island, back when I was a young girl. A fine missionary lady named Rachel took me under her wings and eventually adopted me."

"Well, that's some story," George concluded.

Just as their conversation came to an end, down the cobblestone path came a little girl whose bushy pigtails bobbed up and down. "Mommy," she yelled.

"What in the world is going on? Why are you yelling so loudly?" asked Angel.

"I won the game. I was playing hopscotch with the other girls, and I won!"

"Well, congratulations, young lady," answered the tall handsome man who at that point was a total stranger to Miracle. "My name is George. What's your name?"

"Oh, let me do the honors. That's my daughter, Miracle. Please forgive her disruption. The girls got boundless energy," Angel replied.

"Not to worry. She was just being a little girl doing what they do best," George replied.

"Miracle, come sit and rest a bit. Here, drink some water and cool off," said Angel with all of her maternal instincts aglow.

"I'm sorry, Mr. George."

"No need for an apology. She's beautiful."

"Thank you, and thanks again for fixing my shoe for me."

"It was my pleasure."

"Well, Miracle and I need to be getting on our way."

"Angel, is your name, right?"

"Yes, sir, it is."

As George garnered up some energy, he replied, "Well, I'd like to talk to you sometime or perhaps we can have a bite to eat, if I may ma'am." Angel, completely taken by his good looks, kind gesture, and polite conversation, wasted no time responding. "Yes, I'd love that."

"May I have your telephone number?"

"Yes, you may. It is…" The exchange occurred so smoothly; it was like watching butter melt on a hot potato.

Two days later, George and Angel went to supper. He'd found the sweetest little café on the north side of the island, where the food was to die for. Granted, it was a bit of a ride, but George, ever the gentleman, made certain Angel's ride was as comfortable as possible.

The night seemed to flee quickly. It was obvious they were smitten, rarely taking their attentions in any other direction than each other. Hours passed and the moon made her appearance; romance was in the air, and neither seemed to mind.

Now George, the worldly kind, knew how to wine and dine a lady. He knew how to get from first to second base without striking out. Angel, aware of his smooth abilities, remained true to her focus. "Can we be honest with each other?" Angel asked while taking a deep breath as she spoke.

"Sure, what's on your mind?"

"Miracle is my daughter, and I love her to pieces. She is, however, the product of rape."

"I'm sorry. I didn't know."

"Yes, I know you had no way of knowing. But there is something else you need to know. As a result of that unkind act, I was infected with the HIV virus. I receive treatments regularly, but I have to be very careful. I won't go into details unless you want to hear them."

"No, that won't be necessary. I don't want to upset you," George gingerly responded.

"Miracle and I will be returning to the States soon," Angel explained.

"I don't know exactly how much time you'll be remaining on the island, but I'd like to see you again."

Without hesitation, she replied, "Yes, I'd like that too."

As time for their departure drew near, George and Angel appeared to be inseparable. They attended chapel together, went to dinner regularly, and enjoyed picnics with Miracle down at Kate's Bay.

Now, Pastor Jim's watchful eye was working overtime as he promised Rachel he would make sure they'd be safe. "Angel, seems you've taken a liking to that young man. What's his name?"

"His name is George. He's a pilot. He works for Island Airlines," Angel replied.

"Is he married or have a family hiding somewhere?"

"No, sir, he doesn't. I've been assured."

"Well, if you don't mind, I'm going to make some calls. Just wanna make sure he doesn't. I promised your ma Rachel I'd look out for y'all, and I'm a man of my word."

With a slight smile, Angel thanked Pastor Jim. "I appreciate that."

The time on the island went by so quickly. Before Angel knew it, the day of her departure had arrived. Her summer internship had been a success, and she had found the love of her life in George. Angel couldn't believe it happened for her. He loved her so much, and he loved her Miracle too.

"Mommy, is Mr. George coming with us...you know, when we go home?" Those were among the questions Miracle had roaming about in her little mind.

"Well, to begin with, our flight is tomorrow afternoon."

"What about Mr. George, is he coming with us, Mommy?"

"No, Mr. George isn't coming with us, Miracle."

"Awe, Mommy, I like him. Can't he come home with us?"

"Well, Miracle, things aren't that cut and dry. He has a job and other responsibilities here on the island. It's not that easy to go off somewhere when you have responsibilities at home. Do you understand now?"

"Yes, Mommy."

"I know how you feel. I wish he were coming too." Angel smiled.

It was a bit unusual that her Miracle took a liking to George. That didn't happen all that often. In fact, Terri had been the only person she'd quickly gotten so attached to. It just wasn't her nature to quickly get attached to someone she hardly knew.

"Mommy, there's someone at the door knocking."

"Alright, I'll get it."

It was George. "My dear, I have news."

"What kind of news?"

"I'm piloting your flight back to the States, and I've been given permission to vacation there for two weeks." Before she realized it, into George's arms Angel ran and planted a kiss on his lips that screamed, "Yes!"

"What's that for?" he asked, as though he didn't already know.

"That's the best news I've heard all day!"

"Yes, it is. I love you, babe."

"I love you too, George!" It was now official. George and Angel had fallen madly in love with each other, and public declarations of that kind were just the beginning of what was to come.

"Babe, let me tell Miracle."

"Alright. She"s in her room packing."

"Miracle, sweetheart."

"Is that Mr. George?"

"Yes, this is Mr. George. I have some news for you." Angel peeked around the corner to see what was going on.

"I'm coming with you and your mom."

"Mommy, is he really?" her happy little voice screeched.

"He is." Right then and there, something wonderful happened. The beginning of a strong bond had begun to form; they had become like family.

The flight home was more exciting than anyone could have imagined. Angel smiled all the way, waiting for any appropriate opportunity to brag on her handsome pilot honey bunny. Pastor Jim sat back and watched the festivities, wearing delight like a garment.

Waiting on their arrival at the airport was Rachel and Terri. As usual, the gate was filled with anxious faces, open arms, and grateful hearts. Since Pastor Jim had called ahead to give his Mrs. a heads-up, she quietly hid in the corner, not wanting to miss any of the festivities. Miracle was the first to deboard the plane, then Angel.

"You made it safely," yelled Rachel and Terri in perfect harmony while holding balloons for their girls.

Pastor Jim by then had deplaned as well. He and his Mrs. were all ears, not wanting to miss any part of what was about to take place.

"Yes, ma'am we did. The internship went well too. But I have a special surprise for y'all."

"Surprise! Are y'all okay?"

"We're fine, but there's someone who wants to meet the two of you." As this distinguished-looking gentleman peeked around the corner and made his approach like a fancy jet scoping out its runway, Rachel suddenly remembered him. "Ma Rachel, Uncle Terri. Please meet George." Needless to say, Rachel was thrilled, and Terri was in shock. He was a bit protective of Angel and Miracle, and the thought of anyone moving him out of his comfy spot was none too exciting.

"What's your name again, young man?" he roared in his lion-like voice.

"My name is George. I'm a friend of Angel and Miracle and now hopefully you and Ms. Rachel."

"Hmm, well, Angel didn't let us know you were coming. It would have been good if she had."

"Oh, don't mind Terri. He's a bit protective. Terri, could you please behave yourself," Rachel smized in her younger sister voice.

"Ma'am, there's something you need to know," George responded quite mannerably.

"What might that be?"

"Well," as he takes a moment and clears his throat. "Well, ma'am, I love Angel and Miracle very much. We spent a great deal of time together on the island, and I couldn't stand the thought of being apart from them. I had to come and meet her family."

"Wow, that sounds kind of serious, Mr. George."

"Angel, is something else going on that we need to know? You said the internship went well. Is that right?"

"Yes, ma'am, that's right."

"Well, Terri and I are happy to have you. I assume you've made other accommodations?"

"Well, no, ma'am, I didn't. But I can."

"The ride home is about seven miles. When we arrive, perhaps we can enjoy a cup of coffee, some refreshments, and some good conversation."

"Yes, ma'am, I'd like that very much."

The ride home was a quiet one. Terri was sulking, and Rachel was thinking. George had his arm around Angel, and Miracle was loving the balloons her Uncle Terri and Ma Rachel brought her. "Well, we've arrived home. Terri, please help them get their bags into the house."

"Alright, I guess I can do that," Terri growled.

"You have a lovely home, Ms. Rachel."

"Thank you. It was passed down to us from our grandmother. We love it."

"Angel, perhaps the room upstairs in the attic might be suitable accommodations for Mr. George now that I think of it."

"Yes, Ma Rachel. I think he'll like that. George, there's a room upstairs in the attic that might do. It would save you the trouble of going to a hotel."

"Yes, I would like that very much," George responded. "Ms. Rachel, you need not worry about me. I wouldn't do anything to tarnish Angel's good name. My momma taught me to be a gentleman."

"Now that's what I'm talking about. You must have read my mind, young man," Rachel responded.

"Yes, that is good to hear," Terri replied while his chest struck a position of pride.

"Supper is in an hour. I hope you're hungry because I made all your favorites."

"Aw, Ma Rachel, I love you."

"Miracle, come help me and your uncle set the table, alright?"

"Yes, ma'am, I'm coming."

The dinner table looked especially good that night. Rachel lit her favorite candles and used her expensive china saved only for special occasions. In the center of the table was a large turkey browned to perfection. To its right, a honey-glazed spiral ham with cloves lined up like tiny tin soldiers, and then there was the tray of Cornish hens stuffed with cornbread and sausage stuffing basted in an orange glaze sauce. The side dishes of macaroni and cheese, collard greens, red beans and rice along with some string beans sent Angel's appetite into overdrive. One look at George's face said, "Hmm, good."

George, the gentleman that he was, gently pulled out Ma Rachel's chair and then Angel's. His mannerly ways were especially on point that night. Even Terri took notice. Miracle was so well behaved. She remembered all the table manners she had been taught and was polite too. Angel was so proud of her. The kitchen table talk was just general. Too much detail in front of Miracle just wouldn't do. So everyone waited patiently for her to turn in so the grownups could discuss the obvious—George and Angel

"Ms. Rachel, the meal was delicious. Can I help clear the dishes?"

"No, of course not, you're our guest. I wouldn't think of asking you to do dishes. Terri and I will tidy up the kitchen later on. For right now, he and I would like to hear from the both of you."

"Sure, ma'am, that's understandable. Well, to start, Angel and I met again on the island while she was attending Bible college and doing her internship at Open Arms. Quite honestly, she and I were immediately smitten. I don't know how it happened so quickly, but we fell in love, nearly at first sight, and we spent as much time together as we could. I'm aware of her health challenges and how that came to be, but I love her no less. In fact, I admire her courage, and I believe Miracle is a miracle from heaven. She"s the sweetest thing ever. To be perfectly honest with you, I want to marry them. I want Angel to become my wife, and Miracle my little girl. You see, my wife and son died in a swimming accident some years ago. My son was just a beginner and was told not to swim in the deep water. Well, one day, he got adventurous, and he did. When my wife noticed him out on the waves, she dove in to help him. But the strong undercurrent took them under...both of them. She never reached him, and they drowned. While I was in flight, the news came to my copilot. He waited until we landed safely and then informed me my wife and son had passed away. It was devastating. It's been five years now, and I still get misty eyed when I talk about it. Now, I feel like God has given me another chance to have a beautiful wife and family, and I don't want to mess things up. I know Angel's health challenge is not her fault, and I don't mind the risk because I love her and I know she's worth it.

"I'd like to thank you and Mr. Terri for rescuing my Angel and being by her side through all that she's gone through. I'm not a teenager and neither is she. We are both adults now. We have strong feelings for each other. We want to be together. We want to marry. So I'm asking your permission for Angel's hand in marriage."

"Wow, that was quite a lot. I had no idea you were a widower. I'm sorry for your loss, but at the same time, I'm glad you and Angel found each other. As for me, you have my permission. Now, as for my brother, he'll have to make his own decision, you understand?"

"Yes, ma'am, I understand."

"Well, George, I think I like you. I believe you love my Angel and will protect her and Miracle. If you sincerely want to marry her, you have my permission."

"Thank you, Mr. Terri."

"You can call me Uncle Terri. I'd like that very much."

"Alright, Uncle Terri." Laughter could be heard throughout the house. It was a night to remember.

"Angel"—George dropped to one knee, staring at her with those dreamy eyes—"will you marry me?" Without hesitation, Angel blurted out a huge "*Yes*, I'll marry you, George." Rachel and Terri both produced a thunderous applause that woke Miracle from her sound sleep.

"What's going on, Mommy?"

Tears flowed as that million-dollar smile blinded poor Miracle. "Well, I just got myself a husband and you got yourself a father!"

"Really?"

"Yes!" as Miracle ran into the arms of her new daddy. Her outward burst of energy screamed, "I love you, daddy George," and the deal was sealed.

There hadn't been a happier time in their home since the days when Grandma wore her old aprons filled with family stories and tales. As Rachel walked through those old French doors, she somehow knew grandma could hear the jubilance and the laughter in her heavenly quarters.

Sunday morning arrived, and it was time George met the congregation so lovingly cared for by Pastor Jim. "Good morning, congregation. We have a special guest with us today. Someone we'll probably get to see again. His name is George, and he's an airline pilot. He was kind enough to get us back to the States safely. But aside from that, he and Angel are now engaged to be married. George, please stand as the congregation welcomes you." The applause was thunderous, and the congregation's roars were enormous. George smiled from ear to ear, while Angel looked like an angel. She simply glowed. "Congregation, Angel also managed to complete her Bible college internship too. Now, let's congratulate Angel." The hugs were flying and a ton of tissue too. It was a mixture of tears and smiles, all lending their approval of what was happening for George, Angel, and Miracle.

The next week went by quickly. It was filled with outings, picnics, trips to the mall, and more. But George had to return to the island. It was home to him. For Angel and Miracle, it wasn't an easy good-bye because they had grown to love one another deeply. Needless to say, there were lots of tear-stained eyes and tough good-byes only a broken heart could understand.

CHAPTER THIRTEEN

Wedding Bells Are Ringing

The wedding was just a month away, and Angel's excitement had yet to diminish. She beamed with pride, and she wore it well. Though most brides consider the planning stages to be daunting, Angel did not. She handled it with such grace and ease, as if the busyness was no bother. Each day, she tackled her to-do list with the tenacity of a mother lioness, letting nothing get in the way of her successful catch. On the prowl she was. She had to have the right dress, the right venue, the right caterer, the right florist, the right photographer, and the right accessories. Everything had to be just right. A perfectionist she was. She had dreamt of this day, never really expecting it to happen. So she vowed her wedding day would be special. No last-minute thrown-together wedding for her. Her special day would be one for the books.

Each evening, as she settled down from the day's duties, her phone would ring. It was always George on the other end breathing the fresh aroma of romance. He never failed to lend his support, loving Angel the best way he knew how. Rachel tried to steer clear of their conversations but couldn't. More than once, she found herself eavesdropping because she enjoyed listening to the love birds laugh, talk, and plan their big event. It gave her a thrill like no other. After all, it had been years since she'd heard that kind of romancing. Rachel's own wedding was so long ago she had forgotten how much fun it had been to plan. But one thing was for certain, Angel and George knew that feeling all too well and were madly in love, enjoying every minute of it. Each day, Angel would give him the rundown of what she had been able to accomplish, giggling all the while. They had no issue with public displays of affection, and Miracle loved that. She would go to school telling all her friends, "My mommy and new daddy smooch a lot," and she would say it with a smile in her voice. Of course, her classmates would respond like any other school-aged child, screaming, "That's gross!" while wearing a frown that said a skunk just walked through the room.

Together, Angel and George planned every step of their big day. They chose their bridal party, picked every flower, planned each part of the menu, and decided on wedding favors. By then, the dresses had been ordered, the tuxedos had been altered, fitting the guys to a tee, and everything else was on course, except one thing.

The expenses were adding up, and a mountain of debt had formed quite the tab, not to speak of the telephone bills! George and Angel's budget had burst at the seams, especially the cost of their long-distance telephone conversations. They were about to put Terri in the poor house, but he didn't complain, which was quite unusual. To the contrary, he was as happy as a bug in a rug. Anytime Rachel offered to help out, he would say, "I got this!" In Rachel's book, that meant no thanks. Apparently, he was feeling kind of liberal, and that was fine by her. Rachel was loving her brother and his reformed ways because the old Terri would never go for this kind of thing. He was kind of stubborn and set in his ways. He wouldn't share much of himself and would tell you outright "My retirement pension is mine, and mine alone." He made that very clear to his sister Rachel, especially while they were renovating Grandma's place. But it was obvious Angel and Miracle had indeed stolen his heart.

"Angel, how are things? I know the *big* day is approaching. Y'all handling things?" Terri lightheartedly asked.

"What do you mean?"

"I mean, could you use some help covering the cost of the wedding?"

"Oh my goodness, yes, Uncle Terri!" said Angel with a heaping helping of glee in her voice. "George is going to be so happy. We didn't know how we were going to pay those bills. Thank you so much for helping out!"

August 17 was just a week away, and things were falling into place quite nicely. George was flying in his mother on the sixteenth, and everyone was excited, especially Angel. This would be their first time getting to know one another, but Angel was worrying herself about it a bit. "Why George would wait until the day before the wedding to fly in with family is beyond me," Rachel thoughtfully mentioned.

"Maybe he wants to surprise Angel with a special gift or something, I don't know," Terri responded. "He said he didn't want to see Angel the day before the wedding. Something about it being bad luck."

"Well, I don't go in on that bad luck stuff," Rachel quietly said.

"Yes, I know," Terri concluded.

CHAPTER FOURTEEN

Oh No!

"Ma Rachel, I just spoke with George, and everyone has boarded the plane. Just five minutes to take off."

"Sounds exciting."

"It is! George said he'd call again before the flight takes off."

"Good grief, girl, have you eaten any decent food lately? All I've seen you eat is junk food. You're gonna need your strength, and donuts aren't the healthiest choice you know…"

"Yes, ma'am, I know."

"Weddings can be stressful, and those kinds of treats aren't gonna do the trick."

"I know, Ma Rachel, but the rehearsal dinner is tonight. I promise I'll eat some real food. Okay?"

"Well, only if you promise. You know, I can go in the kitchen and whip up a vegetable omelet."

"No, that won't be necessary."

"Alright. Well, tell George I can't wait to see him later on this afternoon."

"Okay, Ma Rachel. By the way, I have to stop by the caterers and the DJ to finalize a few things."

Angel's excitement never seemed to diminish. She wore it well. "Miracle, I picked up your dress yesterday. It looks simply precious. Please do not touch it! You understand your mommy?"

"Yes, ma'am, I understand. Mommy, don't leave yet. The phone just rang."

"Answer it. If it's your daddy George, tell him to hold on. I'll be right there."

"Hello, this is George. Miracle, is that you?"

"Yes, daddy George. Mommy said hold on, she'll be right there. Okay?"

"That's fine."

Angel hurried to the phone. "How's my favorite pilot?"

"He's very happily in love with you." He knew how to turn on the charm, and he did it well. "We're on the runway, waiting for clearance for takeoff."

"I'm happy to hear that. Babe, please be careful and remember I love you."

"I love you more. Until this afternoon," George swooned. In the background, noises from the control tower could be heard. Angel knew it was time to go.

The caterer, the DJ…I'll run by their offices on the way to the nail salon. I shouldn't be very long. I haven't the faintest idea why either of them would want to see me today! We've already discussed everything. Let me give them a call, she thought to herself.

"Hello, my name is Angel. I'm getting married soon. You called requesting I stop by the office. Is everything alright?"

"Why certainly, everything is just fine. I called because your uncle came by and dropped off a check. But it was for the wrong amount. He paid us $500 too much. I wasn't sure how you'd want to resolve it. That's why I requested you stop by today."

"I was beginning to wonder if something had gone wrong. I'm actually relieved. Well, why not wait and see if additional folks show up for the reception. We may not need to do anything if they do. Just apply the overage to cover the extra meals if there are any."

"Thank you, Ms. Angel. That solved that situation."

"Well, if there isn't anything further…"

"No, ma'am. We resolved that minor glitch. Thank you, Ms. Angel."

Aboard the small private jet were George and his mother. She hadn't ever been to the United States, so this felt like a real treat, almost like getting a two-for-one deal—a wedding and a vacation all wrapped into one.

"George, what's it like, you know, the United States?"

"Very nice, Momma. I think you'll like it a lot. Sit back and relax. I'll have you there in no time."

"Alright, son."

George was no stranger to jets, large or small, because that's what he did for a living, and he enjoyed it very much. The flight was relatively smooth with very little turbulence. However, three and a half hours into the flight, George began getting messages from the control tower warning him of a strange storm boasting 70-mph winds, lightning, and golf-ball-sized hale. It had somehow slipped up on meteorologists without warning. But George had been a pretty confident pilot, and the news didn't appear to alarm him very much. After all, it wasn't like he'd never flown through bad weather before. But for some reason, his copilot began to show some concern. I guess it was the bumpy weather that set his teeth on edge. So as proper protocol required, they alerted their flight attendants to prepare the passengers for a rough ride. And a rough ride it was.

Meanwhile back home at Stateside, things were heating up a bit. "Angel, there's a call for you, someone from Island Airlines," Rachel cautiously announced.

"Island Airlines, why would they be calling me?" Then and there, Angel's instincts peaked, and her nerves jumped into overload. She knew something had gone terribly wrong. She melted onto the sofa, looking as lifeless as a corpse.

"Is this Angel, George's fiancé?" the voice on the other end firmly asked.

"Yes, this is Angel."

"I'm sorry, ma'am, but George's plane was struck by lightning. We lost contact with their flight, and we are unsure of the plane's actual location."

"I'm sorry, sir, you must be mistaken. George and I are getting married tomorrow. Everything has been planned. You must be mistaken," she repeated.

"I'm sorry to be the bearer of such unwanted news, ma'am, but we have no idea of the plane's whereabouts."

The emptiness of Angel's eyes told her story; Rachel and Terri knew something had gone terribly wrong.

"Angel, is George alright?" Rachel asked.

"No. The control tower doesn't have a clue where his plane is." Angel sank further and further into a disparity no human should ever know.

Over in the corner near the sofa stood Rachel. On her face was the look of shock and disbelief. However, she knew she had to keep it together for the sake of Angel and Miracle. She regurgitated the news in her head over and over again yet unwilling to believe it to be true.

"Terri, could you come close. I need your support right now." Rachel's trembling voice testified of her deep pain.

"Airline officials say George's plane was hit with lightning, and they don't know where it is."

"What? They must be mistaken."

"No, Uncle Terri, that's what they told me," said a sobbing Angel.

"Rachel, what else did they say? They must know something! Let me speak to them. What's their number? They can't be getting the story right," bellowed Terri.

"Uncle Terri. I'm telling you that's what they said. They said a storm came out of nowhere, and when they notified George, he had pretty much flown right into it."

"Dear Jesus," Uncle Terri grunted as he fell into his recliner.

"Angel, what would you like us to do? Shall we call the caterer and notify them something unexpected has happened?" Rachel asked.

"No, everything will go on as planned. They'll find my George," Angel replied.

By then, Miracle had meandered into the room. She had been playing video games upstairs in the attic and had no clue what was really going on.

"What's the matter? Why is everyone crying?"

"Come, Miracle. Sit with me for a moment. I have something to tell you," said Rachel as she struggled to regain her composure. Rehearsing those words was not something she wanted to do, but someone had to. So as Miracle sat on Rachel's lap, it was just moments until Miracle melted in her arms like a candle worn from the warmth of its own heat. The news was too much for her.

"Ma Rachel, what are we gonna do? They have to find daddy George. They just have to."

Rachel looked into her eyes, but there were no words to comfort her.

"The best any of us can do is pray and wait to hear from the officials," Terri said in a voice that penetrated their hearts. So they gathered themselves together in one circle as Rachel led them in the Lord's Prayer. At the time, it was all she could think of, and she knew He understood.

The waiting was almost unbearable. Hours passed, and no one talked or even looked in each other's direction. It was a silence to which no one had been accustomed, gut-wrenching to say the least.

"Come, we must get ready for the rehearsal dinner."

"Yes, I agree," Angel chimed in while washing her tear-stained face.

As for Terri, well, now that was another story. He was glued to his recliner; his expression said he had just about checked out of life. He didn't have children of his own, and Angel had become the daughter he never had. Shock and disbelief had taken hold of him, numbed him, and disabled him.

"I'll stay and wait for news. If I hear anything, I'll give you a call, alright? Go on now. Try and have a good time."

"We'll do our best, Terri. When people ask for George, we'll just say his flight got delayed. No one needn't know what's going on…not just yet. Is that okay, Angel?"

Angel had no argument. In fact, it was like she wasn't even there. An hour later, they managed to pull themselves together and left for the restaurant. Miracle stayed behind to keep close watch on Terri, and he on her. The festivities went on without a hitch. Rachel's announcement that George's flight had been delayed surprisingly got very little feedback. No one thought to question it because flight delays happen all the time. The food was good, the music festive, and everyone had a fine time. Angel wore her best smile, though her thoughts were with her beloved George.

"Ma Rachel, I'm gonna ask the caterer to fix plates for Miracle, Uncle Terri, George, and his momma."

"Good idea, I'm glad you thought of it."

That night, Angel wore bravery like a coat of honor. She put on her best face and was as cordial as ever. She greeted her guests, enjoyed some good conversation, and acted as though all was right in her world. She did it impressively while everyone remained clueless about the day's events.

The night's event went by smoothly, and before you knew it, the last guest had departed. Then it happened; the restaurant manager came with a message to call Terri at home. Angel and Rachel both thought it might be best to wait until they arrived home to find out what it was about.

They only lived a short distance from the restaurant, but the ride seemed endless. No one spoke a word; the quietness was almost deafening. As they walked into the house, Terri appeared to be of a different spirit, one whose identity they had not yet determined. "The coast guard called a little while ago. They located the fuselage. According to them, the plane exploded upon impact and everyone perished."

Angel dropped to her knees while Rachel held on to her by a mere thread. Terri paused for a moment and said, "Everyone except George and his momma. She was wearing a life jacket. He found a piece of the fuselage and what was left of someone's seat belt. He used it and tied her to the fuselage, then they held on for dear life. Because they were close to Miami, someone saw the explosion and contacted the coast guard. They located the fuselage and rescued them."

Angel, exhausted from all the drama, sat on the floor and gathered what was left of her emotions. "Uncle Terri, where is he?"

"According to the coast guard, he's been flown to a hospital about fifty miles from here. They are sending someone to escort you there."

"Thank you, Uncle Terri. Can you watch Miracle for me?"

"Sure, we'll have a great time together. You go now and tell your handsome man and his momma we're praying for them."

"Yes, I'll tell them. Ma Rachel, I need you. Can you please come along?"

"Sure."

There was little time for Angel to get dolled up because within minutes, a knock came on the door. "Hello, I am Captain Logan Miller from the United States Coast Guard, and I am here to escort Ms. Angel to the hospital. Your fiancé, George, has been asking for you."

"Thank you. I'm Ms. Angel, and this is my momma. Her name is Ms. Rachel, but we call her Ma Rachel."

"Yes, he asked about Ma Rachel too," replied Captain Miller.

"She'll be accompanying me tonight," added Angel.

Though the hospital was less than an hour's ride, the trip seemed never ending. There had been no official disclosure or information about George's condition, just that he survived the crash and was alive. Neither Angel nor Rachel had any idea what to expect. When the limousine pulled into the emergency room entrance, Angel's heart raced as if it were competing for a thoroughbred championship. Two men wearing white coats walked from behind the emergency room doors and approached the limousine. Their appearance alone frightened an already-nervous Angel.

"Well, ma'am, we can take you to his room. The doctors will speak to you then."

"Thank you."

Angel and Rachel entered the hospital as they wore a strange kind of nervous confidence. Because in their hearts, they had already prayed George and his momma would be alright. The walk through the hospital corridors were reminiscent of times past at Open Arms. The scent of cleaning products and disinfectants were everywhere. As Angel attempted to step into his room, a nurse reminded her she needed to "suit up," so she did. She took one look at his bruised face and bandaged limbs and nearly fainted. He looked nothing like himself.

"George, can you hear me? This is Angel."

He turned his head slightly to the right, looked up at her, and burst into tears. "They're gone. I couldn't save them. I tried, I tried," he cried. Angel had never seen George in such a state. He had never been an emotional man, not at all. She struggled to find the right words; never had she the need to before. Angel quickly turned away so he would not know how deeply pained she was.

"Ma Rachel, please come in," Angel beckoned. Rachel peeked through the door; the smell of disinfectant made it all real to her. Mr. George, bandaged from one end to the other, immediately recognized her.

"Ms. Rachel…"

"Don't try to speak too much just yet. Rest yourself. There'll be plenty of opportunities to make use of that smooth voice of yours," she said, trying desperately to lighten the mood.

"I heard you crying outside in the hallway. The good Lord knows you tried. There wasn't anything you could do about it. Rest yourself now. Let the doctors help you. Alright? You know I love you and always will. We'll get through this, I promise."

"Listen to her, George. She knows what she's talking about," declared Angel. Wisdom flowed from Rachel's lips plenty of times before, and this time was no different. With a slight smile and one tear under his chin, Angel saw a bit of her babe shining through the pain.

"As for your momma, she's resting right now. Doctors say she has a few bruises, that she'll be fine," said Angel as she made her best effort to calm him further. "Miracle and Uncle Terri send their love too. By the way, the rehearsal dinner was a smash hit! We told everyone your flight got delayed, and no one asked questions. Can you believe that?"

"Thanks, Ms. Rachel. I appreciate that you covered for me. I wouldn't want folks to be worrying 'bout me, ya know. Angel, the ceremony is tomorrow, what do you want to do?" George asked. Angel paused for a moment as she reminded herself George had just suffered the loss of several passengers and his crew.

"Well, I'll let you decide. What's it gonna be?"

"My momma wants me to be happy, and I do too. So how about we move the wedding to the chapel here at the hospital? The reception can go on as planned. We don't need to move that."

"I'll make the necessary calls while Angel talks to your doctors," Ma Rachel chimed in.

"Babe, if that's what you want, we can do it," a willing Angel confirmed.

"Alright, if that's what you want," George concluded.

CHAPTER FIFTEEN

It's a New Season

As Angel stepped outside his hospital room, a rather short, thin gentleman wearing a white jacket stopped for a moment to speak with her. His hair was slicked back with all kinds of gel, styled in the most youthful way. However, his hospital badge verified his presence as a member of their staff. As he reached forth to shake her hand, Angel quickly introduced herself.

"Hello, I'm Angel, George's fiancé," she said in a quiet voice.

"I'm the hospital resident who was on call when your friend arrived. He sustained some pretty bad cuts and bruises, you know."

"Yes, but he is a fighter, and I'm glad he is. We've been planning our wedding for weeks now. He has been so excited about it and about his momma flying in for the festivities."

"I know. He kept asking for her…how she was doing."

"Well, obviously, the current situation puts a bit of a damper on things. But George and I still want our ceremony to go forward tomorrow. We've talked about moving it to the hospital chapel with just a few close friends and family members. They would love to witness the occasion."

"Ms. Angel, I agree, that would be a great thing to do. I can help make that happen for you if you'd like."

"Really? Thank you. I'm a bit concerned about George. Can he handle all the attention and the goings-on that weddings sometimes bring? Is he going to be up to it?"

"He'll be fine. The hospital will provide one of those fancy wheelchairs, and his medications will help ease any discomfort he may experience. Not to worry, ma'am. We"ll see to it he's well cared for."

"Thank you."

George hardly knew what day it was. I guess the sedatives were more powerful than he had expected. Terri stayed the night at the hospital to keep close watch; he said George slept through the night except a couple of times when he mumbled a bit in his sleep.

The next morning, however, the nurses could hardly believe his behavior. "What's for breakfast? I'm hungry, and it's my wedding day," were the words that flew through his lips. "I need to look good for my bride but not on an empty stomach! Who's coming to help me?" To say his nurse was surprised would be an understatement. She didn't know whether to run in the opposite direction or call for backup.

"Sir, a male nurse has been assigned to assist you 'cause your uncle has to get ready for the ceremony. He'll help you get showered and shaved," the nurse replied.

"Thanks," said a thankful George.

By now, everyone had heard about George's plight. Calls and well wishes were coming in from every direction. Oddly enough though, for Angel, time slipped into reverse…in slow motion. But she took it all in stride. *Just another case of the nerves*, a voice penetrated her thoughts. For the little orphan girl whose past was soiled with darkness and pain, the day was almost too perfect, too good to be true, and Angel didn't want to do anything that would jinx it.

Twelve noon arrived, and the chapel was filled with happy onlookers. Family, friends, and hospital staff came to witness the happy occasion. The flash of flicking cameras was almost blinding as George's momma was wheeled into the chapel. Angel managed to set aside every sad and fearful emotion brought on by the prior day's events; they were tucked away in a special place where no one could access them. Dressed in her simple gown of ivory lace with a slight twig of baby's breath neatly tucked in her hair, she was beyond happy, through the moon you could say. There in his wheelchair, bandaged from head to toe where body parts peaked through occasionally, was her George. At first glance of his bride, he was simply smitten. He could hardly bare the pain of looking away. His devotion was pure; it was true.

It was precisely 12:05 p.m., when Terri walked his Angel down the aisle. Her radiance could not be hidden from anyone. Miracle was her momma's flower girl, and she did her job well. In the wake of the plane crash, Rachel and Terri cancelled a few things, including all the floral arrangements. At the last moment, they had to pull magnolias from branches outside the front porch window just so Miracle would have something beautiful to toss. Angel had her very own rhythm, her own stride, only something a bride could experience. There was no denying it—she was a happy girl, and they were a lovely couple.

As onlookers watched in anticipation of the nuptials, Pastor Jim proudly read each their vows. George's smooth tones could be heard down the hallway as he vowed to love, protect, and honor his new bride. It was a sight to behold. As he gingerly lifted himself from his wheelchair and kissed his new bride, it was as if he gently transitioned into something so beautiful only someone in love could understand its depth and meaning. It was much more than a kiss, but the culmination of what God had ordained. The sighs of approval were loud and unrelenting. There wasn't a dry eye in the chapel. Everyone could sense Angel's joy. It was deep; it was strong. She and her beloved were finally one.

Now Rachel was elated and offered them all the love she had in store. She was so proud of Angel and how she had dealt honorably with the pain of her past. Every word Rachel uttered for the remainder of that day spoke volumes of her true feelings and deep appreciation that God had brought things full circle. It had opened a well of emotions within from her past, from when each of her daughters experienced their wedding day. Though they were now living their lives in Germany with their military husbands, it was as if they were present with her that very moment.

With Miracle alongside, Angel and George seemed to float through the events of that day. They entered a new phase of life that, for so long, had evaded them. Though Angel sometimes felt she had been cheated out of the happiest days of her life, she never let that alter who she was. She remained true to her faith, and she never let go.

For the remainder of her days, she honored the love of her life as they watched Miracle grow into a blossoming young woman. Pastor Jim was there when they welcomed the addition of an adopted son, and he welcomed their willingness to serve together at their church. Their testimony was filled with highs and lows, of pain and victory, and blessed those who listened.

Now, Rachel was getting on in years. The thought of retirement began crossing her mind. She had been a nurse more years than one could remember and had organized the Room for women who had experienced some less than good things. She loved the residents at the Room; they had been her "babies" for a while now, and Angel had been her right hand, and very good she was.

"I've been thinking on retiring, retiring as director of the Room."

"Really? Ma Rachel, who would do your job?"

"Quite honestly, I thought about you."

"Me?"

"Yes, you. I think you would be perfect for the job."

"Wow, I'm honored."

"Pastor Jim and I have talked about this for a while now. That's why we suggested you go to Bible school. Do you remember?"

"Yes, ma'am, that was a while ago, but I remember."

"Well, I believe the time has come. I must move on." As tears met under Rachel's chin. "I want you to take up the torch."

Angel wept while remembering the path her life had taken. But they were tears of joy because she had somehow survived.

"What can I say, Ma Rachel. I believe God was preparing me all along. I'll never be able to replace you. But I promise to do my best." Angel took a long deep breath, turned to Rachel, and said, "I guess you can say I accept."

Now, when a contented Rachel lay down to rest, her prayer is filled with joy and thanksgiving.

ABOUT THE AUTHOR

Adrienne has worn many hats during her times. She is wife, mother, and grandmother to her loving family as well as teacher to her young students. She is a people person, whose love of learning has yet to diminish. She has a benevolent spirit and makes every effort to impact the lives of those plagued by economic challenges. Her love of music is quietly woven into every fiber of her existence and has brought her great joy.